"You enjoyed the kiss we shared last night as much as I did."

Parker leaned closer to Shelby as he separated her fingers against his chest with a single slow stroke of his own fingers and twined them together, still holding her hand against his heart. "Last night as you lay alone in your bed, you wondered what it would feel like if you could shed all of your inhibitions—all of your guilt about being with another man—and just let yourself go with me."

Parker's words took Shelby completely by surprise. Her confusion showed in her tawny eyes.

A corner of his mouth lifted. "Honey," he said, "I know you're afraid of getting hurt, and you have no reason to trust me. But don't shut me out because of what happened to your husband. I know you miss him. But he's gone and I'm here. Give me a chance. Give yourself a chance...."

Dear Reader,

Thanksgiving is the one holiday in the year where the whole family gathers for that traditional turkey dinner with all the trimmings. And who can resist just one extra helping of stuffing or pumpkin pie!

Silhouette Romance novels make perfect Thanksgiving reading. They're a celebration of family and all the traditional values we hold so dear. *And* they're about the perfect love that leads to marriage and happy-ever-afters.

This month we're featuring one of our best-loved authors, Brittany Young—not to mention the ever-popular Arlene James and Marcine Smith, and the talented Pat Tracy and Patti Standard. And to round out the month we're continuing our WRITTEN IN THE STARS series with the passionate Scorpio hero in Ginna Gray's *Sting of the Scorpion*. What a lineup! And in months to come, watch for Diana Palmer, Annette Broadrick and *all* your favorites!

The authors and editors of Silhouette Romance books strive to bring you the best in romance fiction, stories that capture the laughter, the tears—the sheer joy—of falling in love. Let us know if we've succeeded. We'd love to hear from you!

Happy Reading,

Valerie Susan Hayward
Senior Editor

BRITTANY YOUNG

Lady in Distress

Silhouette Romance

Published by Silhouette Books New York

America's Publisher of Contemporary Romance

To Tara, the best editor a writer could ask for.

SILHOUETTE BOOKS
300 E. 42nd St., New York, N.Y. 10017

BRITTANY YOUNG

lives and writes in Racine, Wisconsin. She has traveled to most of the countries that serve as the settings for her books and finds the research into the language, customs, history and literature of these countries among the most demanding and rewarding aspects of her writing.

All underlined places are fictitious.

Prologue

Shelby stood motionless near the edge of the old New England cemetery, a small bouquet of flowers clutched in her hand. Trees in full summer bloom shaded the graves, a gentle hush seemed to have fallen over nature. Even the birds were silent.

She took a deep, strengthening breath and slowly exhaled. Her high heels made no noise as she walked across the short, springy grass to a grave marked with a pale blue marble headstone.

Shelby's heart caught as she knelt beside it. Her husband had been gone for nearly a year, but it never seemed to get any easier. Time was supposed to be the great healer, but it wasn't working its magic on her.

Leaning the bouquet against the headstone, Shelby reached out and tenderly traced the name carved into the polished surface. *Eric.*

The cool breeze blew a lock of tawny hair across her full lips, but Shelby didn't notice. Leaves rustled, interrupting the silence. She didn't notice that, either. Shelby was lost in her thoughts.

A woman watched from the spot where Shelby had stood before, her dark eyes pained at the heartache of her dearest friend. She looked at her watch and waited a few more minutes before crossing to Shelby and touching her shoulder. "Shelby, we should be going now if you want to catch your plane to Texas."

Shelby turned her head and looked up at her friend with eyes the same tawny color as her hair. "Oh, Katy," she whispered in a husky voice.

Katy was swallowed by a feeling of helplessness. "I know. I miss him, too." She knelt in front of her friend. "Shelby, maybe you shouldn't have taken this assignment. Let the magazine get someone else to cover that Texas murder trial."

"I can't. I already told you, it's not just any murder trial. I knew the woman who was killed."

"Not all that well."

"No, but we both wrote for *American Profiles* at one time or another and crossed each other's paths. She was a wonderful writer."

"And now she's a wonderful story," Katy said cynically.

"I know that's how it looks, and maybe for the magazine that's the way it is. But I liked Diane, and I'd really like to follow her husband's trial."

"Do you know him?"

"I met him once or twice. He was—and I suppose he still is—quite wealthy. He had a habit of popping up wherever Diane happened to be working. I don't think he trusted her to be faithful to him, though I don't know why. She seemed to love him very much.''

"So you've met him. Do you think he's capable of murdering his wife?''

"To tell you the truth, Katy, I thought he was a jerk. But a murderer?'' She shrugged her shoulders.

Katy looked at her for a long moment. "Do you think you can cover the trial without prejudice, Shelby? I mean, what with your being acquainted with Diane and all.''

She nodded. "It's a concern, I know, but I really think I can, or I wouldn't have accepted the assignment.''

Katy sighed.

"What's wrong?''

"All of this talk about the trial and your work is well and good, but completely beside the point.''

"And the point is?''

"You! You need to take some time for yourself. You haven't since Eric's funeral. You've just gone from job to job.''

"Oh, Katy,'' she said tiredly, "time to do what?''

"To grieve. To begin some kind of recovery. Maybe even get yourself some professional help in handling Eric's death and your future.''

"I'm still functioning. As far as I'm concerned, that's handling it.''

"But there's more to life than just functioning. You deserve to be happy again, Shelby.''

Shelby gazed at the headstone. *Happy*. She couldn't even imagine what the word meant.

Katy turned Shelby's face toward her own. "Honey, you're only twenty-five years old. You have your whole life ahead of you. I know how much you loved Eric, but he's gone and he isn't coming back. You have to face that fact, and then you have to start your life over without him."

"Not yet."

"Shelby..."

"I just can't. I need more time."

Katy sighed. "All right. But if you don't do something about your life pretty soon I'm going to start interfering. And you know what that means." She arched her eyebrows. "Blind dates!"

Shelby smiled wanly. "Thanks for trying to cheer me up. I don't know what I'd do without you."

"You'd be late for your plane," she said with a smile as she rose and pulled Shelby to her feet.

Arm in arm, the two women strolled through the cemetery to where Katy's car was parked. "Believe it or not," Katy said, "one of these days you're going to fall in love again. There's some man out there just waiting for you."

Shelby shook her head. "No. I've had more than enough pain for one lifetime."

"Loving someone doesn't necessarily lead to pain."

"But there's always that risk." Shelby's voice was soft.

"Anything worthwhile involves some risk."

Shelby glanced sideways at her friend. She'd known Katy since childhood, and they'd always understood each other so well. But this was something Katy couldn't understand, as hard as she tried. Katy had never lost anyone close to her. Once a person's life is touched by death, things are never the same. Every moment of happiness, no matter how brief, is tainted with guilt.

Shelby was twenty-five years old, but inside she felt eighty. Life was no longer something to look forward to. It had become an ordeal to simply get through as best she could, one day at a time.

"Oh," Katy said to her across the car roof as a thought suddenly struck her, "have you gotten any more of those phone calls recently?"

"I got one last week."

Katy shook her head in disgust. "Did he say anything this time?"

"Just my name over and over again in that strange whispering voice of his." She looked at Katy with troubled eyes. "Sometimes when he calls me he doesn't say anything at all. There's just the eerie sound of wind." She shivered. "It's weird."

"I'm telling you, Shelby, this guy knows you from somewhere. He didn't pull your name out of the phone book."

"I know."

"You'd think that after almost a year of these calls, the police would have found out something about him."

"I don't know what more they can do, Katy. They've spoken to every man with whom I've had even the most inconsequential contact and come up empty. They've traced some of the calls, and all they've learned is that the man calls from pay phones."

"And you don't have any idea who it might be?"

"Believe me, I've thought and thought. I just don't know anyone who would do something like this."

"Does he frighten you?"

"He shouldn't, I suppose. I mean, he's been calling all these months and hasn't done anything to hurt me. But yes, he frightens me. He's obviously unbalanced or he wouldn't be doing this in the first place."

"I wonder what he really wants?"

"I don't know, but I almost wish he'd just come out and say it. Then perhaps I could figure out how to deal with him."

"Maybe he just wants to hear your voice."

"I wish I could believe that. I really do. But my sixth sense tells me that's not it."

They opened the car doors and climbed in, neither aware of the man standing twenty yards away with his hands jammed in his trouser pockets, watching.

As soon as the car had left the cemetery, the man strolled casually to Eric's grave. Picking up the bouquet of flowers Shelby had left behind, he removed a small white carnation and tossed the rest aside. He raised the flower to his nose and inhaled its delicate fragrance. It reminded him of Shelby.

His Shelby.

Staring at the headstone, he rhythmically drew the soft petals back and forth across his cheek as a smile twisted his mouth. "Soon, Shelby. I'll be coming for you soon."

Chapter One

Shelby drove down the parched main street of Dry River Falls, Texas. There weren't any stoplights—probably because there wasn't enough traffic to justify having them installed, she surmised. There were perhaps only three thousand people in Dry River Falls, and most of them lived and worked on the large ranches outside of the town.

She had to admit that the town was charming. Very hot and a little dusty, but charming nonetheless. The tiny downtown area was like something out of an old-fashioned western. The main difference was that the street and sidewalks were paved.

She drove around the town square—a small area shaded by trees. There were benches, obviously newly whitewashed, and a small fountain that sprayed clear water into the air.

Just beyond the square was the combination courthouse, jail and county prosecutor's office, a three-story whitewashed adobe structure. And across the street from the courthouse she found The Hotel. She smiled when she saw the sign. Since it was the only hotel in town, she supposed it didn't really need a name. It was a five-story, very ordinary, brick building.

All of the parking spaces in front of The Hotel were taken up with rental cars—her colleagues, no doubt, here to cover what promised to be a rather sensational trial. Shelby drove around the corner and squeezed her own rental car between two others. There was no doorman, of course, so Shelby retrieved her own luggage from the trunk and carried it into the hotel and across the surprisingly spacious lobby to the front desk. The clerk, a man in short sleeves and no tie, looked up at her with a friendly smile. "Yes, ma'am, what can I do for you?"

"My name is Shelby Chassen. I've booked a room with you for the next several weeks."

"Here for the trial, eh?" he asked conversationally.

"Along with dozens of other writers, apparently," she said with a smile.

"Yes, ma'am. They've been coming in for the past few days. Aren't you with some magazine? I think I took your reservation myself."

"American Profiles."

"Right. I've heard of that." He thought for a moment. "Why, I think I might even have read it once." He handed her a postcard-size form to fill out and a pen. "Isn't that the same magazine Diane Lyle wrote for?"

"Yes, it is."

"So you knew her?"

"Not particularly well, but yes, we were acquainted."

The man shook his head. "She was a fine woman. Just a fine, fine woman."

"Do you know her husband, Jefferson Webster Lyle?"

"J.W.? Sure. Everybody knows everybody here."

"Do you think he murdered his wife?" she asked as she filled in her name and address on the form.

"Well, ma'am, I just don't know. He's got a temper, no question about that. But maybe he is telling the truth, and she was already dead when he found her."

She slid the form to him across the desk.

"Thank you, Ms. Chassen. I'll need a credit card."

Shelby took one from her wallet and handed it to him. "Has Mr. Lyle's attorney arrived yet?"

"You can say that again. Jerry Fisher and his people have taken over almost the entire fifth floor." He made an impression of her card and gave it back to her.

"I'd like to leave a message for him, if that's all right."

"Sure." He picked up a pen and poised it over a notepad.

"Jerry," she dictated slowly, "I'm covering this trial for *American Profiles*. I'd appreciate your talking to me about this case. I'd also like to speak with your client. I'm staying at the hotel. And then just put my name at the bottom.''

The clerk finished the note with a flourish. ''I'll see that he gets this right away.''

''Thank you.''

He handed her a key. ''Now, if you need anything, you just call me. My name is Bo.''

''Thank you, Bo.''

''You're in room 315. There's an ice and soda machine down the hall. The restaurant is open for breakfast and dinner but not lunch. Breakfast is served from five-thirty until ten, and dinner is from six o'clock to eleven. It's not fancy, but it's good food.''

Shelby smiled at him as she picked up her suitcases and carried them to the only elevator. After pressing the button, she stood directly in front of the doors, lost in her thoughts. She wasn't at all sure that Jerry Fisher was going to cooperate with her. She'd followed an earlier trial of his, and the resulting article had been something less than complimentary.

The elevator doors slid open, and Shelby absently forged ahead—at least until she crashed unexpectedly into a solid wall of chest. Strong hands reached out to grip her shoulders as her suitcases fell to the floor. ''I'm so sorry,'' she gasped as she looked up into a tanned face with two of the bluest eyes she'd ever seen.

The grooves in his cheeks deepened. ''I'm afraid you took the brunt of the collision, ma'am,'' he said, his voice a slow, gravelly drawl that sent a pleasant vibration through her. ''Are you all right?''

Shelby stepped away from him and averted her eyes. "Yes, I'm just fine. I should have been more careful."

He picked up her suitcases and set them into the elevator for her. "Can you get these to your room on your own? They're kind of heavy."

Her mouth smiled, but it didn't reach her eyes. "I got them here all the way from Vermont. I think I can manage the next fifty or so feet on my own. Thank you, anyway."

The Texan lifted a dark brow. Her tone and her manner were polite enough, but she seemed to dismiss him. He wasn't used to that from women.

Shelby pressed the button for the third floor and waited, very aware of the man's eyes on her. When nothing happened, she pressed it again.

The Texan stayed where he was, staring at her, willing her to look back at him. It became almost a challenge.

The doors began to slide shut. In the split second before they closed, Shelby raised her tawny eyes to his. Her look was cool, distant.

He stared at the closed doors for several seconds, then shook his dark head. The woman was wrapped in ice. And yet...

As far as Shelby was concerned, what was out of sight, was out of mind. When the elevator doors closed, leaving the Texan on the other side, she pushed him from her thoughts. He made her uneasy, and her way of dealing with that was not to think about him.

When she got off the elevator, she found her room about halfway down the hall. It wasn't fancy, but it had a great deal of charm, with its large four-poster bed and old-fashioned furniture. There was also a small sitting room with a couch, some comfortable chairs and a table set in front of a large window that looked out on the street. She could even see the courthouse. It was a perfect place to work. There was no television, but there were two telephones, one in each room.

She spent an hour unpacking and putting things away, then pulled from her shoulder bag a large envelope her editor had forwarded to her in Vermont. It contained information about the case she would be covering, starting with jury selection tomorrow morning. She'd gone through the information a couple of times on the plane, and now she walked into the sitting room, organized the papers into small, neat stacks on the table and went over the case history one more time.

Jefferson Webster Lyle was a man who had inherited a great deal of money from his oilman father. He'd never actually accomplished anything on his own. His résumé was littered with failed business deals, extravagant spending and lots and lots of women—both before and after his marriage to Diane. He had lived a very public life in which every bar fight and every physical confrontation with his wife was chronicled with great delight by the press. He had many homes in many places and didn't spend much time at the ranch he'd inherited in Dry River Falls. But a little more than a year ago both he and Diane were at the ranch. According to J.W., as he liked to be called, they'd had one of their frequent arguments.

He'd stormed out of the house to drive around the ranch. He didn't see anyone and no one saw him. When he'd returned to the house several hours later, he claimed that he'd found Diane, dead. She'd been shot. When the police had examined the guns from his extensive collection, they discovered that one was missing. A few days later they located it at the bottom of a creek on the property. It was the murder weapon. J.W. was arrested on the spot and he'd been in jail ever since.

Shelby made her way through the press clippings one more time, amazed by the volume. The man seemed to have missed no opportunity to tell his story or get his picture in the papers and magazines.

The defense was already trying its case in the media, which didn't surprise her. That was the way Jerry Fisher worked. The facts weren't nearly as important to him as the theatrics. There was article after article of Jerry Fisher touting his client's innocence, claiming J.W. was a good ol' boy, a victim of circumstances, a grieving husband mercilessly harassed by a publicity-seeking prosecutor who was trying to make a name for himself.

And from the prosecutor, Parker Kincaid, there was only a terse "no comment" in response to reporters' questions.

Shelby put everything back into neat stacks. With a weary sigh, she leaned back in her chair and gazed out the window.

She was so tired.

It seemed as though she was always tired lately. It was because of the insomnia she'd had ever since Eric's death. No matter how exhausted she felt when she went to bed, she was never able to sleep through an entire night.

Tears stung her eyes. God, she missed him. He'd been her best friend.

The phone rang.

Shelby turned her head and stared at it. Jerry must have gotten her note. Wiping away the tears with the tips of her fingers, she cleared her throat and walked to the phone. "Hello?"

No one answered.

"Hello?" she said again, more firmly. "Jerry, is that you?"

Her only answer was the sound of the wind.

What little color there was drained from Shelby's face. She put the receiver back in its cradle and stared at it with frightened eyes. Him! How had he known where she was?

Shelby took several deep breaths to calm herself. She wouldn't panic. Nothing bad had happened during all of the months she'd been getting the phone calls. She had to remember that.

She took one more deep breath and slowly exhaled. Normalcy was the key. It was time for dinner, so that was next on her agenda. Going into the bathroom, she splashed cold water on her face and dabbed it off with a towel, barely bothering to look at herself in the mirror. Picking up her purse and a small pad of paper to make notes on, she went downstairs to the restaurant.

It wasn't very large. There were only perhaps fifteen tables, most of which were already occupied. Shelby looked around, saw a few familiar faces and smiled her greeting, but made no move to join anyone. The hostess seated her at a table that had been set for two people and removed one of the place settings. "Can I get you something to drink?" the young woman asked in a thick Texas accent.

"Just a mineral water, thank you."

She took a pen from her purse and sat staring at her blank notebook. No matter how hard she tried not to let it, the phone call kept creeping into her thoughts. Shelby resented that as much as the phone calls themselves. She couldn't be worrying about that when she had so much work to do.

And she wouldn't. She wouldn't let that cowardly caller have that kind of power over her.

With a resoluteness that wouldn't have surprised anyone who knew Shelby well, she pushed the problem from her thoughts and began organizing herself for the task ahead.

One of the first things she needed to do was talk to Jerry Fisher. Jerry was brash and bold and very East Coast. Most of his clients were high-profile people like J. W. Lyle who could afford his outrageous fees. He was famous for his theatrical courtroom performances—and for getting his clients off the hook. Shelby wasn't fond of his methods, but she liked him as a person.

The prosecutor, Parker Kincaid, was someone she'd never heard of. She'd need to get some background on him, but she couldn't imagine there would be much to find. How good an attorney could he be if he'd ended up working for a county with a population as small as this one? He'd probably never tried a case this important before, and she'd be willing to bet he'd never come up against an opponent as capable as Jerry Fisher. It was hard not to write him off before the trial even began.

"Shelby? Shelby Chassen?"

Shelby looked up from her notepad to find Jerry Fisher standing over her, tall, blond and blow-dried to perfection.

"I got your note. I knew *American Profiles* was sending someone to cover this trial, but I rather hoped it wouldn't be you," he said dryly.

"That doesn't sound very promising for my article." She held out her hand with a smile. "Hi, Jerry. How are you?"

He took her hand and held it for a moment. "Despite what I just said, it's nice to see you, Shelby. I heard about your husband. I'm really sorry."

"Thanks, Jerry." Shelby didn't want to talk about Eric with Jerry or anyone else. She quickly changed the subject. "So how about it? Can I talk to you about the case? Perhaps get an interview with your client?"

"What's in it for me?"

She met his look with a direct one of her own. His tone was teasing, but she knew how serious this was to him. "Just fair coverage of what's going on in the trial—which you'll get even if you don't talk to me."

"That's not much of an incentive."

"It's as good as it gets, Jerry."

He shook his head. "You're tough on a man's ego. When I get too puffed up about myself, all I have to do is pull out that piece you did on the Cameron trial. Ouch!"

She couldn't help smiling. "It wasn't that bad."

"You skewered me, my dear."

"I skewered you accurately, though."

"True. But skewering is skewering, and it seems more painful when it's accurate."

"I'll take that as a compliment."

He smiled at her. Jerry liked Shelby, but he couldn't claim to know her very well. She kept her own counsel better than anyone he'd ever met. "Are you expecting anyone to join you for dinner?" he asked.

"No. As it happens, I'm all alone."

"Would you mind if I did?"

"Not at all. But if you don't object to my asking, where's the rest of your entourage?"

Jerry sat across from her. "The others are eating in the suite while they get ready for jury selection tomorrow morning."

"Why aren't you?"

"I'm as ready as I'm ever going to be—and I needed to get away from them for a little while."

"Is it your usual group?" At the trial she'd covered, Jerry had never entered the courtroom without a co-counsel, an expert in jury selection, an investigator and a secretary.

"Some of the faces are different, but the job descriptions are the same."

"How do you think that will play here?"

"Play here? What do you mean?"

"Jerry, this is Dry River Falls, Texas, not Manhattan. Your entourage might be impressive in the big city, but out here a jury might just feel sorry for the prosecution for being so overwhelmingly out-gunned.''

Jerry shook his head and grinned. ''Overwhelmingly outgunned. I like that. But seriously, I don't think it's going to be a problem. I've been at this for a long time and I know what I'm doing.''

The waitress brought Shelby her mineral water and turned to Jerry. ''Can I get something for you?''

He flashed her an utterly charming smile along with a look that seemed to say there was no one in the world he'd rather talk to at that moment than her.

The young waitress's tanned, freckled cheeks flushed prettily in response.

He looked at her for a long moment, causing her cheeks to grow an even brighter pink. ''Just dinner,'' he finally said. ''I'm really hungry.''

''I'll get you a menu.''

As soon as she'd gone, Shelby shook her head in quiet amusement. ''I have to hand it to you, Jerry, you're really good.''

''Thank you. I like to keep in practice. But as I recall,'' he said as he leaned back comfortably in his chair and eyed Shelby, ''the look didn't work on you.''

''I guess I was a tougher sell.''

His gaze moved over her face. Shelby was without question one of the loveliest women he'd ever seen. And one of the smartest. He enjoyed talking to her. ''What about now?''

She sipped her mineral water and set the glass back on the table. ''Now I'm an impossible sell.''

He gazed at her with the same intensity he'd used so effectively on the waitress. "If I've learned one thing over the years, it's that nothing is impossible."

Shelby met his look with a direct one of her own. "I'm not interested, Jerry. Don't be offended. I assure you, it's nothing personal. I'm here to write a story on this trial, and that's all I'm here for."

A corner of his mouth lifted. "All right. I'll stick to business."

"Thank you." Shelby was more relieved than she let on. She just wasn't up to that kind of banter.

The waitress brought both of them menus. Jerry winked at her and followed her with his eyes as she walked away. "So tell me, Ms. Chassen," he said as he opened his menu and began studying its contents, "have you decided on the guilt or innocence of my client yet?"

Shelby smiled. "Why, Jerry, you know me better than that. Besides, like everyone else at this point, I only know what I've read, and that, frankly, isn't much. You have, of course, done your usual blustering to the press, but that doesn't mean what you've said is true."

"Excuse me? My usual blustering?" He was all wounded innocence.

"Oh, Jerry, please," Shelby said with a laugh. "You know exactly how you sound when you talk to the media about your pet clients."

He clicked his tongue and shook his head slowly back and forth. "Oh, boy, I think I see the handwriting on the wall. You're going to hang me out to dry in your article, aren't you, Shelby?"

"Only if you deserve it. Which reminds me that you didn't answer my question about speaking to your client."

"I don't know about that, Shelby. I don't know if that's such a good idea."

"You can be present if you want. I'm honestly not trying to pull a fast one on you, Jerry. That's not my style."

"I know."

"I'd just like to have some personal contact with the man so I can get a feel for what he's thinking, what he's going through."

"I'll have to talk to J.W. Now let me ask you a question."

"All right."

"What are you bringing in the way of personal bias to this article you're doing? I understand you knew Diane Lyle."

"That's right. I've also met J.W. I'm trying very hard not to have an opinion on your client's guilt or innocence. I want to sit through the trial as though I'm a member of the jury and form my opinions based on the evidence presented."

"That's fair enough." He watched as someone passed their table. "Well, well. You're batting a thousand tonight, Shelby."

"What do you mean?"

"The prosecutor just walked in."

Shelby looked up from her menu and saw the same man she'd bumped into earlier striding toward a table in the back of the restaurant. Faded jeans hugged his long thighs. A tan sport coat stretched tautly across his broad shoulders. This was the prosecutor? she wondered silently. He looked like a cowboy.

Her gaze followed him to a table where an older woman was seated with her back to the room. The man stopped behind her and rested a hand on her shoulder. She looked up at him with a wan smile and said something. He responded and walked around the table to sit facing the woman and, incidentally, Shelby.

As though sensing Shelby watching him, his eyes lazily shifted to her. For a long moment, he just looked at her, then he inclined his dark head. Shelby's hand unconsciously tightened on her napkin as she returned the acknowledgement and looked away.

"I think I'm going to have a little Mexican food," Jerry said, still eyeing the menu. "What about you?"

Shelby closed her menu and set it beside her plate. "I'm not very hungry. I think I'll just have a salad."

He signaled the waitress. She came a moment later with a place setting for Jerry. He and Shelby were silent while the waitress arranged everything for him, then he gave her their order. Shelby hardly noticed, so intent was she on the Texan.

"What do you know about the prosecutor?" Shelby asked as soon as the waitress had gone.

"A lot, but not as much as I'd like to know. I did my homework on Parker Kincaid. He used to be a criminal defense attorney in Houston. A good one from what I understand. I talked to some attorneys who worked with and against him, and they had nothing but praise for him. But one day he just quit, left Houston and ended up in this godforsaken place as a prosecutor, of all things, convicting the same people he used to get off."

She tried to glance inconspicuously toward the Texan. "I wonder why he did that?"

Jerry shrugged. "No one I talked to seemed to know. Maybe you can ferret it out of him."

She turned back to Jerry to ask him a question, but her real focus was at the other table. "Do you always research your opposition so thoroughly?"

"Always. It's important to know who you're dealing with in a trial."

Shelby's gaze shifted once more to Parker. Even sitting down he was tall. And quite handsome in a rugged kind of way—if one happened to like that sort of thing. Some women certainly did. Personally she preferred men who looked more refined—like Eric. The prosecutor was listening intently to something the woman was saying. "Do you know who he's with?"

Jerry didn't turn around; he didn't need to. He'd seen the woman earlier. "You bet I do. That's my client's former mother-in-law. I'd introduce you, but as you can imagine, I'm not one of her favorite people right now."

"Meaning what? That she thinks your client murdered her daughter?"

"I'm afraid so. I've tried to talk her around to our side, but without much success."

"So tell me, Jerry," she said innocently, "do you think your client did it?"

Jerry grinned at the casual way she slid the loaded question into their conversation. "Nice try, Shelby.

Very nice. But you forget that I've had dinner with you before. Once bitten, twice shy, as they say."

She smiled back.

A movement at the far table caught her eye. Parker reached out and touched the woman's hand. She looked as though she was crying. Shelby's own smile faded.

Jerry turned his head to see what she was looking at, then he turned back to Shelby with a groan. "Oh, no."

"What?"

"All I need is for her to do that in front of the jury. I'm going to have to find a way to keep her out of the courtroom."

"Her daughter is dead, Jerry," she said quietly. "Of course she's emotional."

"I understand that. But I can't have her grief unfairly influencing the outcome of the trial."

Shelby looked at him unblinkingly. "What about your client's family? I imagine they'll be there in force, showing their support."

"He only has a sister left. Besides, that's different."

"Why? Both situations are ripe for unfairly influencing a jury."

Jerry sighed. "Look. I have to do what's best for my client, and keeping that woman out of the courtroom is what's best. I'm not going to sit here and argue with you about what's fair and unfair in a murder trial."

Parker Kincaid got to his feet. The woman remained seated. He put his hand on her shoulder and quietly spoke to her, then strode toward Shelby and

Jerry. Purposely not looking at him, Shelby willed him to pass on by. It didn't occur to her at that moment that she should have been on her feet grabbing his arm to talk to him.

She felt rather than saw him stop in front of her. With a reluctance she didn't even try to identify, Shelby raised her eyes to his.

"Hello again," he said in the charmingly rough drawl she remembered from before.

"Hello," she said coolly.

"I'm Parker Kincaid. And you are?"

"Shelby Chassen."

He took her hand in his.

She gracefully withdrew it.

Parker studied her with steady blue eyes. "I take it that you made it to your room all right."

"Oh, yes. I'm happy to report that you were my only collision."

Parker turned to Jerry and extended his hand. "Hello, Jerry. Nice to see you again."

Jerry rose and shook his hand. "It looks like we'll be seeing a lot more of each other starting tomorrow. You don't have a case, you know."

The corners of Parker's mouth stretched into a lazy smile. "I guess we'll find that out soon enough." He looked from one to the other of them. "Are the two of you working together?"

Jerry didn't say anything, so Shelby was forced to answer. "I'm covering the trial for *American Profiles* magazine."

"*American Profiles.* That's a fine magazine. It's the same one Diane occasionally wrote for. Did you know her?"

"We'd met."

"I see. Have you written anything for *American Profiles* before?"

"Several times."

"Watch her, Kincaid," Jerry warned. "Guard every word you say to the woman, or else they'll come back to haunt you."

"It sounds as though you've had some personal experience in that regard."

"Oh, yes. Very personal. Would you like to pull up a chair and join us?"

"You mean consort with the enemy?" Parker asked with a half smile.

"Only for a few minutes."

"Thanks, anyway, Jerry, but I can't." He looked at Shelby. "It was nice meeting you, ma'am."

Shelby touched his arm to keep him from leaving. "Mr. Kincaid, I'd like to speak with you about this case when you have the time."

"Everyone calls me Parker."

Shelby looked directly into his eyes which, amazingly, made her seem even more remote—at least in Parker's opinion. "I'm sure they do, Mr. Kincaid, but I'm not everyone."

Parker seemed to smile—and yet he hadn't. There was something in his eyes that made him appear amused. "Everyone and no one, Shelby," he said quietly with a shrug of his shoulders and using her first name with pointed deliberation. "It's all the same, isn't it? What exactly is it that you'd like to speak to me about?''

Her eyes were locked with his. ''The Lyle case, of course. I'd like for you to share some of your thoughts with me about the case as the trial proceeds.''

''That's highly unusual.''

''Not as unusual as you might think. It's certainly not unethical. Do you have a personal problem with it?''

Parker studied her expression closely. He couldn't tell if she was laying down a challenge or simply asking a polite question. She was impossible to read.

''I'll warn you again,'' Jerry said, only half joking, ''that if she doesn't like the way you conduct your case, she'll crucify you in her article.''

Shelby ignored him. ''I'd also like to speak with Diane Lyle's mother. I'm afraid I don't know her name.''

Parker was silent for so long that Shelby wondered if he'd heard her. ''Her name is Jane Mitchell,'' he finally said quietly, ''and if she chooses to speak with you about what's going on, it's entirely up to her.''

''Would you mind if I asked her now, seeing that she's here in the restaurant?''

''It's not up to me to either mind or not.''

''I understand that, but I was hoping you'd have the good manners to introduce us.''

Parker's eyes narrowed. ''For someone who wants a favor, you don't ask very nicely, lady.''

Shelby had the grace to be ashamed of herself. It wasn't like her to be rude. There was something about this man that rubbed her the wrong way. "I apologize."

"Accepted."

"I'll rephrase my request. Would you please introduce me to Mrs. Mitchell?"

"That's much better. Of course I'll introduce you."

"Excuse me, Jerry," Shelby said, rising. "I won't be long. If our food comes, go ahead and start without me." She walked ahead of the Texan toward the older woman.

Mrs. Mitchell looked up at Shelby. Her eyes widened as her breath left her in a gasp.

"Jane," the Texan said gently, "this is Shelby Chassen. She's a writer with *American Profiles* magazine."

Shelby shook her hand. "How do you do? I hope I'm not intruding...."

The older woman just stared at her.

Shelby looked at her quizzically. "Is something wrong?"

"At first glance you look so much like my Diane. Your hairstyle—your coloring." She shook her head. "I'm sorry. Did Parker say you write for *American Profiles?*"

"Yes. I was acquainted with your daughter."

"I see. And now you're covering the trial of Diane's murderer for the same magazine she used to write for. What exactly do you want, Miss Chassen?"

"It's Mrs., but please call me Shelby."

Parker's surprised gaze flew to the simple gold band on Shelby's left ring finger. It had never occurred to him that she was married. His eyes, narrowed now, moved back to her face.

"As you said, I'm covering your son-in-law's trial for the magazine. What I'd like to do is get as balanced a portrait of all of the parties involved as possible. To accomplish that, I need to talk to you about Diane and how you viewed her relationship with her husband."

"I see."

"Do you mind if I sit here?" Shelby asked, indicating the chair next to the woman.

"I suppose it's all right." She looked nervously up at Parker. "You're staying, aren't you?" she asked.

"Sure." He sat across from Shelby, on Mrs. Mitchell's other side, and casually stretched out his long legs.

"I'm really very sorry about what happened to your daughter, Mrs. Mitchell," Shelby said with a quiet sincerity. "Believe me when I tell you that I understand talking about what happened won't be easy for you."

The woman's eyes filled with tears. Jane Mitchell was a pretty woman of about sixty. Her brown hair, streaked with gray, was stylishly short and emphasized her high cheekbones. Grief had etched lines into her pale skin.

Shelby saw the other woman's pain and came face-to-face with her own. She had to steel herself against it, and the only way to do that was to distance herself emotionally. She'd become an expert at doing that. So much so that she didn't even realize any longer that she was doing it.

To the man watching her with deceptively lazy blue eyes, it was fascinating. Shelby came across as cold and unemotional. Detached, even. But Parker had seen a flicker of pain cross her features. He saw the barrier being dropped into place. This was one very complicated woman.

"I appreciate your sympathy," the older woman said. "As you probably know, there's already been a lot of press attention given to this case. No doubt because J.W. is such a prominent man."

"And because he has an attorney who enjoys talking to the press and getting his picture taken," Shelby said.

"Most people seem to be lining up on one side or the other. What side are you on, Mrs. Chassen?" the woman asked.

Parker let his gaze leisurely wander over Shelby. She had the kind of face a man could look at for years and never tire of. Her skin was pale and smooth and looked as though it would be cool to the touch on even the hottest night. His eyes moved over her delicate profile and came to rest on her full lips. No woman with lips like that could possibly be as cold as Shelby Chassen seemed to be.

Or as cold as Shelby Chassen wanted everyone to think she was.

His gaze moved over her eminently touchable silky hair and down her slender throat to her gently rounded breasts.

Shelby was aware of the Texan's eyes on her and shifted uncomfortably in her seat. "I'm not on anyone's side. I'm here as an impartial observer, not as a member of the jury."

The woman thought it over for a moment, then looked at Parker. "I don't know. What do you think?"

He reluctantly looked away from Shelby. "It's up to you, Jane. I expect your former son-in-law will talk to her until he's blue trying to convince her of his innocence."

She nodded. "You're right, of course. He's certainly talked to everyone else. I'll think about it," she said to Shelby.

"Thank you. I can't ask for more than that."

Parker rose. "Jane, I'll see you in court tomorrow. You," he said to Shelby, "walk with me to the lobby." It was an order, not a request.

Shelby looked at him in surprise.

"Now."

Shelby narrowed her eyes at him as she rose. She wouldn't have dreamed of creating a scene, but her feelings about being ordered around were abundantly clear. "Please excuse me," she said to the other woman. "I'm glad to have had this chance to meet with you, whatever your decision."

With her eyes burning a hole in the back of the Texan's head, Shelby followed Parker out of the restaurant.

He stopped abruptly and turned to face her. "Okay, lady, you and I are going to come to an understanding."

Chapter Two

"Excuse me?" Shelby looked at him unblinkingly. "What understanding might that be?"

If there were other people in the lobby, neither of them noticed.

"Jane Mitchell has been through hell. She lost her only child. This trial is going to be difficult enough for her. I don't want you to make it any more difficult."

"I assure you, that's not my intention—"

"I know exactly what your intentions are," he interrupted her calmly. His eyes moved over her face. "You don't care anything about Jane Mitchell or what she's going through. The only thing that matters to you and your publisher is getting the story and making it as sensational as possible."

Shelby eyed him coolly, which was an amazing feat considering how furious she was. "You don't know anything about me or my publisher, if that's what you think, Mr. Kincaid.''

"Not personally perhaps, but I know your type."

Shelby arched a delicate brow. "My type?"

"Your type. You and your cool aristocratic reserve. You wouldn't know an honest emotion if it said your name and slapped you."

She took several slow breaths before answering. "First of all," she said calmly, "I'm not an aristocrat. And secondly, I don't feel I should have to wear my heart on my sleeve to prove to a cowboy like you that I have feelings."

Parker's expression didn't change. His eyes stayed locked with hers. "I'm warning you right now, Mrs. Shelby Chassen, that if you do anything to upset the course of this trial, or to cause that woman more pain, you'll answer to me." He inclined his dark head. "Good night."

Shelby, rarely at a loss for words, watched in inarticulate silence as he walked away.

Jerry chose that unfortunate moment to come out of the restaurant. "Shelby, your salad's on the table."

She whirled around. "I'm not hungry anymore. Just charge it to my room and eat it yourself if you want it."

"Whoa! Are you all right?"

Shelby caught herself. "I'm sorry, Jerry. I just had a little run-in with your opponent. That's no reason for me to take it out on you."

"Don't apologize. That's good news for my side. Stay mad at him. Are you sure you don't want your salad?"

She nodded, calm once again. "I think I'll just go to my room. I'm a little tired. It's been a long day."

"Don't forget your purse. It's still at the table."

"Oh, right." She went back into the restaurant for her purse, then took the stairs to her room.

She could hear the phone ringing even as she put the key in the door. For just a moment, her hand froze, remembering the earlier call. But then she moved again. It might be her editor.

As soon as the door opened, she flipped on the ceiling light and crossed the small sitting room to the telephone. She took her time, putting her shoulder bag on the couch and sitting down, before answering the insistent ringing. "Hello?"

"Hello, Shelby," said the whispery voice.

She gripped the receiver with both hands. "Why do you keep calling me? What do you want?"

"You know what I want."

"I don't. You keep calling and calling. I wish you would just stop."

"I can't do that, Shelby. I won't do that." He took several breaths. "I want you, Shelby."

His matter-of-fact words chilled her. "You don't even know me."

"Oh, but I do. By the way, I really liked that last bunch of flowers you left at your husband's grave. And I liked that dress you had on. That particular shade of blue becomes you."

Her heart missed a beat. "You were there?"

"I'm everywhere you are," he whispered.

Shelby quelled her rising hysteria and tried to keep her tone reasonable. "Please, whoever you are, leave me alone. I've told the police about you. One of these days you're going to get caught. Surely these phone calls to me aren't worth going to jail for."

"I'm not going to get caught. I'm the one who's doing the catching."

"Please..."

"Everything's going to be all right, Shelby. You'll see. One day soon we'll be together. You and me. No one's going to keep us apart."

"Look, you need help. Maybe a doctor..."

"You think I'm crazy?" The whisper grew harsh.

Shelby tried to keep her voice calm. "I didn't say that."

"Good, because I'm not. I know exactly what I'm doing. I want you and I'm going to have you. Eric's gone and it's just you and me."

"No!" Shelby slammed the phone down. She wrapped her arms around herself and rocked back and forth. "No."

It rang again.

"Stop it!" she screamed.

It kept ringing.

She picked up the receiver and slammed it down, then lifted it again and dropped it on the floor.

She had to get out of there. She couldn't stand being in that room another minute. Jumping up from the couch, she went into the bedroom, stripped off her clothes and carelessly threw them onto the bed, then changed into shorts, a tennis shirt, socks and athletic shoes. Pocketing her room key, Shelby went downstairs and through the lobby to the street.

Even at night, the heat mercilessly wrapped itself around her, but she welcomed the discomfort.

She looked up and down the street, wondering which direction she should go. Neither looked particularly promising, so she just turned right and started walking at a slow, steady pace. She tried to force her thoughts in the direction of her work, but the memory of the whisperer kept intruding.

He had no right to do this to her.

She kept hearing his words over and over again.

She walked faster.

Who was he?

She walked even faster.

Why was he doing this to her? What could he possibly be gaining from frightening her?

Shelby broke into a run. She wanted to stop thinking. She had to stop or she'd lose her mind.

She was so tired of thinking.

She ran faster. She got to the end of the main street after just a few blocks, and it changed into a dark country road without sidewalks. Gravel crunched under her feet as she ran on the side of the road, traveling with what little traffic there was. It was a stupid thing to do and Shelby knew better.

She knew, but she didn't care. Not tonight, anyway.

Some cars whizzed past. She didn't notice.

Her heart was pounding so hard it felt as though it was going to explode from her chest. Every breath she pulled into her lungs hurt, and she was glad.

She didn't see the pothole before she hit it. One minute she was running and the next minute her ankle collapsed beneath her, sending her crashing onto her knees and tumbling headlong onto the gravel.

Dazed and winded, she lay where she'd fallen, unaware of a pickup truck screeching to a stop a few yards away. She raised herself to a sitting position, still gasping for breath, dragging air painfully into her lungs.

"What the hell are you doing out here?" drawled a now-familiar voice.

"Oh, no," she groaned as she looked up at the last man in the world she wanted to see at that moment. "Not you again. Go away. Leave me alone."

"Out here in the middle of nowhere? I don't think so." He knelt beside her. "That was quite a spill you took. Where are you hurt?" Parker asked as he reached for her leg.

"Don't touch me," she said, pulling away from him. "I'm fine." Still breathing hard, she rose unsteadily to her feet. "I got myself out here, I can get myself back to town."

"Don't be silly. I'll take you back."

"I'm never silly. And no, thank you." With all of the dignity she could muster, Shelby started to hobble toward town.

"Oh, for heaven's sake, woman, don't be an idiot." Parker swept her into his arms and held her against his chest.

His touch crackled through her senses. Shelby panicked. "Put me down this instant!"

"Stop being so dramatic." Their faces were inches apart. Parker gazed into her eyes as he held her—and then he noticed something he hadn't before. "Why are you trembling?" he asked her quietly.

For a moment, for just one brief moment, he saw Shelby stripped of her cold facade. There was a whole world of emotion in her eyes. And then she looked away. "I'm not," she said as she folded her arms defiantly across her breasts.

"All right. Don't tell me. I expect I'll find out eventually."

Parker carried her to his truck and placed her on the passenger seat. He walked around to the driver's side, climbed in, and without saying anything to Shelby, he put the truck into gear and started driving.

Shelby closed her eyes. She was so tired. The wind from the open window blew over her hot face and lifted the damp hair off her neck.

She opened her eyes a minute later and sat up straight. "You didn't turn the truck around."

"That's right."

"Where are we going?" she asked, her body tensing as she looked out the window.

"My house."

Her heart started pounding again. "I don't want to go to your house. I want to go back to the hotel. Now."

"I have antiseptic and bandages at my house. After I get you patched up, I'll take you to the hotel."

"No! This is kidnapping! I want you to take me back right now."

Parker pulled the truck off to the side of the road and stopped. The fear in her voice wasn't something he could ignore—or understand. "What is wrong with you?" he asked as he turned toward her. "I assure you I have no ulterior motive in taking you to my house. I'm not so desperate for a woman's company that I find it necessary to abduct one off the street. And if I did, it wouldn't be you."

Shelby looked at him blankly for a moment, then laughed. Those phone calls had her jumping at shadows. "I guess I deserved that. I'm sorry."

Parker shook his head. "You sure are changeable."

"I suppose I must seem so to you." She sighed. "Look, it just isn't necessary for you to take me to your house."

"It is necessary. You don't mess with cuts in this part of the world. You take care of them. It's too easy to get an infection. You aren't going to find what you need at the hotel to prevent that from happening. All right?"

Shelby turned her head and stared out the window. "All right," she said in resignation.

Parker put the truck back into gear and drove on the main road for another mile or so before turning onto a one-lane gravel road. The truck bounced and swayed. Shelby gripped the edge of her seat with one hand and the dashboard with the other.

"I'm perfectly capable of taking care of myself," Shelby felt she had to add.

"Oh, yes," he agreed. "I can see that. Running down a strange road in the dead of night is what I personally consider taking really good care of your-self." He parked the truck in front of a white single-story ranch house. Welcoming light poured from the windows and lit a friendly-looking porch. Parker walked around to the passenger door and opened it. "Come on," he said as he put his hands at her waist to help her out.

She let him lower her to the ground, then politely pushed his hands away. "I can walk."

"By all means." Parker stood aside and gestured toward the house with a courtly wave of his hand. "After you, Princess."

Shelby dug her teeth into her lower lip. Her right ankle hurt like hell, but she was determined to make it into the house on her own.

Parker bounded up the steps and opened the door, waiting beside it with exaggerated patience as Shelby limped up the steps.

A woman wrapped in a robe, her long greying hair hanging down her back in a braid, suddenly appeared in the doorway. "What on earth is going on here?" she asked in English lightly accented with Spanish. "My dear," she said as she crossed the porch to Shelby to take her arm, "are you all right? Why aren't you helping her, Parker? She's obviously hurt."

"Mrs. Chassen prefers her independence, Rosa."

"What happened?" the woman asked as she helped Shelby up the steps.

"I fell while I was running."

"Well, we'll have you fixed up in no time."

They walked through a small foyer and down a hallway to the kitchen. "Here," the woman said as she led Shelby to a stool at the counter and pressed her onto it.

Parker crouched in front of Shelby. He cupped the back of her leg with his hands and lifted it so he could check her scratches and her ankle. The woman brought over a bowl of warm water with a clean cloth.

"Rosa," he said as he continued his examination of Shelby's leg, "this is Shelby Chassen. She's writing an article about the Lyle trial. Shelby, this is my housekeeper, Rosa Fernandez."

Shelby smiled at her, but her mind was on Parker's fingers as he probed her ankle.

"Ouch!"

Parker looked up at her apologetically. "Sorry about that. It's not broken, but it might be sprained. We'll pack it in ice for a while and then wrap it in an Ace bandage."

"I'll get one for you," Rosa said.

"No, that's all right," Parker said as he stood up. "You go back to bed. I'm sorry we disturbed you."

"Are you sure?"

"Positive. There's nothing Shelby needs done to her that I can't do myself."

Shelby looked at him with dry inquiry.

Parker grinned. "I probably should rephrase that, but I'm not going to. Is Danny asleep, Rosa?"

"He said he was going to read in bed for a little while, but that was more than an hour ago. I'm sure he's asleep by now."

"Okay. I'll check on him later."

Rosa touched Shelby's shoulder. "Good night. I hope we meet again under better circumstances."

"Good night, Rosa, and thank you."

When the housekeeper had gone, Parker handed Shelby the warm, damp cloth. "Clean up your knees and elbows."

Shelby watched as he went to the freezer and pulled out an ice pack. "Who's Danny?"

He wrapped the ice pack in a paper towel and crouched in front of her once again to hold it against her ankle. "Not that it's any of your business, but he's my son."

Shelby looked at the top of his dark head in surprise. She hadn't really pictured the man as a human being, much less as someone's father. "How old is he?"

"Six."

"And your wife?"

Parker looked up at Shelby with a wry smile. "You want to know how old she is?"

Shelby smiled before she could catch herself. It changed her whole face and gave Parker yet another glimpse at this mysterious woman.

"I'm not married. I never have been. Danny's real parents were good friends of mine. They were killed in a car accident when he was just a few months old. Danny had no other family so I adopted him." With the ice pack in place, he took the cloth from Shelby's hand and began dabbing her cuts with it. "What about you? Do you have any children?"

"No."

"Do you and your husband plan on having a family?"

It took her a moment to answer, and when she did, it was in a whisper. "My husband is dead."

Parker's hand stopped as he looked at her, his expression full of compassion. "I'm sorry, Shelby."

She didn't say anything.

"How long ago?"

"A year."

"What did he die from?"

"An automobile accident." She cleared her throat. "Can we talk about something else?" The last person in the world she wanted to discuss Eric with was Parker Kincaid. He was as different from her Eric as a man could be.

Parker watched her without seeming to as he lifted her arm and gently cleaned her scratched elbow. "I hope you won't go out running like that again," he said without missing a beat.

"I think I learned my lesson."

"What were you trying to do? Nobody runs like that just for exercise."

She was quietly thoughtful for a long moment. She had no intention of telling him about the phone call. "I guess I was trying to make myself tired so I could sleep tonight," she finally said.

"Is that usually a problem for you?"

"Yes," she said without elaborating, and closed her eyes with a sigh. All of her energy seemed to have drained from her.

Parker wrapped his hand around the smooth skin of Shelby's forearm. She was aware of each of his fingers, the light but firm pressure, the warmth.

He gently dabbed her elbow with the damp cloth and then drew it down the length of her arm. With each stroke, her skin grew more sensitive to his touch.

She took a deep breath. He smelled wonderful. Like fresh air.

Her physical awareness of Parker caught Shelby off guard. Her eyes flew open. "I'll finish that," she said as she put her hand over his to stop the movement.

Parker, his face near hers, looked into her eyes. "Did I hurt you?"

"No," she said quickly, looking away. "I'd just rather do it myself."

With a shrug of his shoulders, Parker handed her the cloth and crossed the room to a high cabinet from which he removed a bottle of antiseptic, some cotton balls and an Ace bandage. Kneeling in front of her again, he said, "I'm going to put this bandage on your ankle, then wrap the ice pack around it."

Shelby stared at the top of Parker's head.

"This shouldn't hurt too much," he said as he took off the ice pack and started winding the bandage around her foot and ankle.

His dark hair was thick, with a natural wave. There was a little bit of gray mixed in, despite the fact that he couldn't have been more than thirty-five.

Her gaze moved over the planes of his face and rested for a moment on his well-defined mouth and the intriguing crease in his chin. He had the kind of rugged good looks that stirred a woman's senses, and she hadn't a doubt in the world that he knew it. How could he not? He turned his head slightly, and she found herself looking at the strong line of his jaw and throat.

"There," he said as he fastened the last clip. "How does that feel?"

"It doesn't hurt much at all anymore. It might not even be sprained."

"I hope it isn't, but there's no sense in taking chances with the swelling." He poured antiseptic onto a cotton ball and dabbed the cuts on her knees, then handed it to her. "Here, you can do your elbows. Would you like something to drink?"

"A glass of water would be nice." She looked anywhere but at him.

Parker put ice in a glass and ran some cold tapwater into it. "I'll take you back to the hotel in a few minutes. First I want to check on Danny."

Shelby took the glass from him, watching quietly as he left the kitchen. She actually liked him more now that she knew about Danny.

Looking around the kitchen as she sipped the water, she found it to be really comfortable—a place where a family could gather and talk while they ate or cooked. It wasn't fancy, but it was immaculate.

Sliding off her stool, Shelby picked up the ice pack and carried it with her as she hopped on one foot out of the kitchen and into the living room to settle on a couch.

With a sigh, she leaned back and gazed around the room. Like the kitchen, it was a product of the home's environment—and owner. Earthy colors mingled with different textures; desert tones mixed with Indian influences.

Books lined a wall from ceiling to floor. She would have loved to have seen what Parker Kincaid considered good reading, but at the moment she didn't have the energy necessary to cross the room to examine the titles.

Raising her foot onto the couch, Shelby put the ice pack on her ankle and looked at her watch. What was taking him so long?

Lying back, her head cushioned by the armrest, she folded her hands across her stomach and stared at the ceiling.

All of that running she'd done was having it's desired effect. Everything about her was tired, from her eyes straight down to her toes.

And she felt safe here. Safe to sleep. She let her eyelids drift down for a moment, then forced them open.

They drifted closed again, and this time she simply let them. It was too much effort to open them. Within minutes, her breathing was soft and even.

When Parker came downstairs, ready to leave, he found Shelby asleep on the couch. He reached out to touch her shoulder, intending to wake her, but pulled his hand back. She looked so peaceful that it seemed a shame to disturb her.

Sitting on the edge of the large and solid coffee table, he allowed himself a long, leisurely look at her softly parted lips. What man could look at those lips and not want to kiss them? And what response would there be? Or, more to the point, what response would she allow herself? She tried so hard to be in control, and Parker found her efforts rather endearing. But at that moment, she was completely vulnerable.

Parker rose, took a blanket from the back of the couch and settled it gently on top of her. As he was leaning over to tuck it around her shoulders, Shelby opened her eyes and looked up at him, sleepy and unfocused. Suddenly her eyes opened wide and he could see the panic in their depths.

"It's all right," he said quietly, calmly, as he pushed her hair away from her forehead. "It's only me."

She rose up on her elbows, her eyes still on him. The panic subsided. "What time is it?"

"About midnight."

Shelby sat up the rest of the way. "I've got to get back to the hotel."

"You're welcome to stay here for the night. I'm sure Rosa won't mind. We have a guest room."

She shook her head. "No, thank you. Just take me back."

He shrugged, not really understanding her reluctance when she was obviously exhausted. "As you wish."

When Shelby stood up, she swayed unsteadily on her feet.

Parker put his hand around her waist. "Are you okay?"

She looked up at him, obviously chagrined. "I'll be fine as soon as I get a good night's sleep."

She moved away from his steadying touch and limped outside to the truck. Parker followed, gave her a hand up into the vehicle and leaned over her to fasten her seat belt.

Shelby held her breath until he was finished, pressing herself as far back onto her seat as possible. When Parker straightened away from her, he flashed her a look of mild amusement. "Do you have this reaction with all men, or have you singled me out for some reason known only to yourself?"

"Reaction?"

"Yes. You behave as though you think I'm out to do you some bodily harm."

"You're imagining it."

"The only one here with an imagination problem is you, Shelby." He closed the door and walked around to the driver's side.

Shelby followed him with her eyes. In a way, he was right. She knew perfectly well that Parker Kincaid wasn't going to hurt her. She was just uncomfortable around the man. The logical way to handle that was not to *be* around him.

The fifteen-minute trip from the ranch to the hotel was accomplished in complete silence. When they arrived, Parker came around the truck and helped her out.

"I can make it from here," she said quickly as she stepped away from him.

"I'm sure you can, but I'm going with you, anyway."

"It's really not necessary."

"Look," he interrupted, "I'm walking you to your room. The longer you argue with me about it, the longer it's going to be before you get there, and the end result will be the same."

Shelby sighed. She was too tired to argue. Together they went through the lobby and up the elevator, then down the hall to her room. Shelby took the key from her pocket and unlocked her door. Without looking at Parker, she started to walk into the room. "Thank you for your help."

The telephone rang. Shelby jumped and stared into the room behind her.

Parker looked at her curiously. That wasn't exactly a normal reaction to a phone call. "What's wrong?"

"I thought I left the phone off the hook."

"Off the hook? Why would you do that?"

It rang again, and she made no move to answer it. "Not for any reason that concerns you," she said absently.

"Aren't you going to answer it?"

She looked at him and then back toward the phone as she unconsciously dug her teeth into her lower lip.

"Go ahead. I'll wait."

"No. That's not necessary."

Parker didn't like the way she looked, and he wasn't about to leave. "I'll wait," he repeated as he leaned his shoulder against the doorjamb and crossed his arms over his chest.

Shelby glared at him, but he wasn't noticeably intimidated. "You're impossible," she muttered as she turned on the light and crossed the sitting room. Her hand hovered over the receiver before finally gripping it and raising it to her ear. "Hello?"

"Where have you been, Shelby?" The whispery voice sounded angry. "I don't like it when you go out and I don't know where you are."

Her face went so pale that Parker came into the room and took the phone from her. "Who is this?" he demanded of the caller.

There was only the sound of someone breathing heavily—angrily—and then a loud click as the caller slammed down the phone. Parker hung up and looked at Shelby. "What's going on? Who was that?"

"I don't know." She couldn't cover up the tremor in her voice as she looked into his eyes. "He just keeps calling."

"Have you told the police?"

"Not here, but I did in Vermont. They haven't been able to catch him."

"What does he say? Does he threaten you?"

"He's never actually threatened me, but he's starting to sound . . . possessive."

Parker sat on the arm of the couch facing Shelby and firmly took her hands in his. This was obviously the reason she was so jumpy. "You should have protection."

She shook her head. "I've thought of that, of course, but this has been going on for a year. How long am I supposed to have someone following me around? Besides, the man's never approached me. I don't think he means any harm."

"You don't know what he means. How do you think he knows you're here?"

"I don't know." She looked into his eyes, sounding genuinely mystified. "He seems to find me wherever I go. When he called me earlier today, not only did he know that I'd visited my husband's grave in

Vermont, but he knew what I was wearing and that I'd left flowers behind.''

"So it's more than phone calls. The man is following you. That's not good."

Shelby slid her hands from his. Walking to the window, she looked outside, unable to penetrate the darkness beyond the street, unaware of cold, angry eyes staring back at her. "He could be out there right now."

Parker came up behind her and put his hands on her shoulders. "He might well be. Which is something to think about the next time you decide to go for a run in the middle of the night."

"I know that was stupid of me."

"Fairly. Don't do it again."

"I won't."

"Next time he calls you, you call me."

Shelby turned around and looked up at him. "I appreciate your concern, Parker, but this isn't your problem."

"I'm making it my problem."

"That really isn't—"

Parker cupped her chin in his hand. His eyes roamed over her face. "If you tell me one more time that it isn't necessary, I'm going to..."

He hadn't expected to do it, and Shelby certainly wasn't expecting it when he lowered his lips to hers. It was such a natural gesture that at first she responded without thinking, parting her lips softly beneath his. But as the kiss grew slowly deeper, with Parker drawing her into it—into him—she pushed her hands against his chest.

Parker raised his head and looked down at her. "I've been wondering since the moment we met what you'd be like to kiss," he said softly.

Shelby, embarrassed by her own reaction, backed away from him. "Would you mind leaving now? I'm really very tired."

"Shelby, I . . ."

"I'm very tired."

He knew not to press her. "All right. I'll see you in court tomorrow." Parker walked to the door, turning back to her just before leaving and meeting her eyes. Without saying anything, he closed the door behind him.

She had to get away from here. Katy was right. She should have taken a vacation instead. Maybe it wasn't too late.

Going quickly into the bedroom, she picked up the phone and dialed her editor's home number. "Come on, Peter," she said after the second ring. "Come on."

Someone at the other end fumbled the receiver. "Yeah?" answered a sleep-filled voice.

Relief flooded through her. "Hi, Peter. It's Shelby."

"Shelby?" There was a long pause. "What time is it?"

"I don't know. Midnight. Maybe a little later. I'm sorry if I woke you."

"That's okay. Are you calling from Texas?"

"Yes. I got here earlier this evening."

"Terrific. So you're all settled in. Have you made any contacts yet?"

"Yes," she said absently. "Listen, Peter, I'm calling because I want you to send someone else to cover this trial."

"Someone else? You've got to be kidding. Why?"

She could hear his sheets rustle as he sat up in bed. "I just can't do this. Surely there's someone else..."

"What do you mean you can't do this? This kind of writing is your forte, Shelby. Plus you knew Diane. That's why I chose you in the first place," he said.

"I'm not talking about the writing."

"Then what? What else is there?"

"It's personal."

"You'll have to be more specific."

Shelby was silent for a moment. "I can't."

"Well, it doesn't matter. You could have the best reason in the world and I still couldn't do what you're asking. I would if I could, you know that. But the trial starts tomorrow. There *is* no one else. You were the writer I chose and you agreed to do it."

Her heart sank.

"Shelby? Are you still there?"

She nodded as she sank back onto the bed. "Yes, Peter, I'm still here."

"I'm really sorry, Shelby."

"I know."

"If you want to take a long vacation after this story's finished, no problem."

Shelby sighed. "I shouldn't have called you, Peter. I was being impulsive."

"Don't worry about it. Are you going to be all right?"

"I'll be fine. Just forget we even had this conversation."

"Consider it forgotten. And by the way, I'm sending a photographer to take some companion pictures to go along with the article. I think you've worked with him before. Charles Greene."

"Yes. He's good. When's he coming?"

"Not for a couple of days. I figure he can get the shots he needs then as well as now."

"Okay."

"Anything else?"

"No."

"Good. I'm going to go back to bed. Good night, Shelby."

"Good night, Peter." Shelby replaced the receiver, then lay back and stared at the ceiling.

Who was she kidding? She didn't want to leave because she needed the rest.

She raised her fingertips to her lips.

She wanted to leave because of Parker Kincaid.

Parker pulled his truck alongside his house and stopped. He didn't go directly inside, but sat on the porch. The only light came through the living room window.

There was no point in going to bed. He'd never be able to sleep. The reason was Shelby Chassen. She intrigued him, and he was a man not easily intrigued.

Chapter Three

After another sleepless night, Shelby was up early. She wanted to get a good seat in the courtroom. Without paying too much attention to her clothes, she pulled out of her closet a multicolored blue skirt, blue short-sleeved T-shirt and sandals. Her ankle felt a little tender, particularly if she moved it a certain way, but she could get around just fine with an almost unnoticeable limp.

As soon as she walked out of the comfort of the air-conditioned hotel, the Texas heat covered her like a blanket. Another woman journalist who had the same idea as Shelby about getting there early, swore softly. "I wonder if anything interesting is going on in Alaska?" she asked Shelby rhetorically without breaking stride.

Shelby smiled, but didn't even try to keep up with her as she crossed the street well behind the other woman and made her way into the old, Spanish-style courthouse.

There were a few people in the foyer, all reporters—she could tell by the way they were dressed—none of whom she knew. Shelby stopped in front of the directory and found that the courtroom she was looking for was on the second floor. She also discovered that Parker Kincaid's office was on the third floor, and that the jail where J. W. Lyle, Jr., was being held was in the basement.

There was no elevator, so Shelby walked up the wide staircase to the courtroom. Standing just inside the open double doors, she looked around. There were only a few people scattered throughout. Shelby chose a seat toward the middle of the courtroom, where she'd have a good view of everyone involved in the trial. Pulling a legal pad and pen out of her shoulder bag, she got herself ready, then really studied her surroundings.

It was an old room in an old building. The wood floors clearly showed decades of wear. The church pew seats could easily have been the originals, with the stain worn off in places and initials carved into some of the armrests. A gigantic wooden ceiling fan turned lazily over head, barely stirring the still, hot air. The arched windows set in the white stucco walls were open, but instead of helping, they seemed only to let the hot air inside.

If it was this bad at eight o'clock in the morning, Shelby could just imagine what it was going to be like in the afternoon. Already she was hoping for a short trial.

As the minutes passed, the courtroom filled with people and the low, steady hum of conversation. A few people Shelby knew stopped to say hello, but mostly it was every man for himself.

Above the hum, there was a flurry of activity at the door. Shelby turned in her seat and watched as Jerry Fisher entered the room with his group following closely behind. The three men were nearly indistinguishable in their Italian suits and blow-dried hair. She recognized the slightly heavyset man as George Gregson, Jerry's investigator, and the other man as Bob Johnson, one of Jerry's law partners. The two women had precisely the same shade of blond hair, moussed to perfection, and both were dressed in suits with short skirts. The slightly taller one was Dr. Carol Hindes, a psychologist and expert in jury selection. The other woman was no doubt Jerry's secretary. They looked as though they'd come straight from the pages of a magazine telling women how to dress for success. None of the five Easterners had done anything to try to blend in with their Texas surroundings, and Shelby couldn't help but wonder if they weren't making a mistake.

A deputy came through a door at the front of the courtroom. A step behind him was Diane's husband, Jefferson Webster Lyle. His fashionable dark suit blended in perfectly with his defense team. Only the handcuffs and ankle chains set him apart. He was perhaps thirty years old, very handsome and clean-cut, just as she remembered. He certainly didn't look like a murderer. As Shelby knew very well, that was a big strike against the prosecution. Juries tended to be more forgiving of good-looking defendants.

Jefferson laughed at something one of the deputies beside him said. Shelby found that strangely disquieting. Whether he was guilty or not, his wife had been murdered. His carefree attitude was inappropriate, to say the least.

When the group reached the defense table, one of the deputies removed the prisoner's chains and took up a guard position at the side of the room.

Jerry, always meticulous about his appearance, managed to look cool and starched even in this heat. There wasn't a wrinkle in his suit or a bead of sweat on his high forehead.

He turned in his seat and smiled at Shelby, then leaned toward his client and said something. The defendant raised his eyes, looked right at her and winked. Then he said something to Jerry that made the attorney laugh. Jerry left his group and walked back to her. "Hello, Shelby."

"Hi, Jerry."

"I talked to J.W. about the article you're writing. He says he might be willing to talk with you."

"I hear a 'but' in there."

"He'd like some guarantees."

"Such as?"

"He wants to make sure that if he cooperates with you, you'll show him in a favorable light to your readers."

"Jerry, you know I can't agree to something like that. What if I sit through this trial and in the end feel he's guilty?"

"You won't, believe me. This guy is being hosed by both the police department and the prosecutor's office. All of the evidence is circumstantial."

"That's not for me to decide—at least as far as what I write is concerned."

"Well, without that guarantee, I don't think J.W. will talk to you. He thinks, and I believe he's justified somewhat, that because of your working relationship with his wife, you're already disposed to see him convicted."

"Believe me, Jerry, that's not the case. What were his other conditions?"

"He wants to read the finished copy and make any changes he sees fit to incorporate."

Shelby shook her head. "Again, that's completely out of the question."

Jerry shrugged. "Okay. I'll tell him."

"You might also mention that if he does decide to cooperate, the article will be much more balanced than without his help."

"Do I sense a veiled threat in there?"

"Not at all. You know perfectly well that with or without his help, I'll be scrupulously fair in reporting the facts."

"I'll tell him that, too."

Jerry started to leave, but Shelby caught him by the arm. "What was it that Lyle said to make you laugh when you told him I was here?"

"After he saw you, he just said that he'd forgotten how attractive you are and that if and when he gets out of this mess he's going to look you up."

Shelby couldn't hide her distaste, but Jerry didn't notice because he was already on his way back to the defense table.

And then came Parker Kincaid.

Shelby felt him enter rather than saw him. Turning slightly in her seat, she watched as he walked unhurriedly through the courtroom, a stack of files under his arm. He wore his dark suit carelessly, as though he'd thrown it on with little thought. The top button of his shirt was undone and the knot in his tie was loosened. His long, dark hair still looked a little wet from the shower. You'd never catch this guy using a blow dryer, Shelby thought with a private smile. He sat alone at the prosecutor's table—quite a contrast to the crowded defense table.

As though he sensed Shelby staring at him, Parker turned his head. His blue eyes locked with hers and narrowed as his look unwaveringly pinned her against her seat.

Shelby looked back at him with a direct gaze of her own, unable to do anything else. She was physically frozen.

And then he released her.

Shelby took a deep breath and stared down at her trembling hands.

A soft current of air hit her as a young woman walked past with Jane Mitchell. The older woman sat immediately behind Parker, while the younger one leaned over the railing separating the observers from

the participants to speak to Parker. He talked quietly.
She nodded occasionally. He scribbled something on
a sheet of paper and handed it to her. Turning to leave,
the young woman glanced at Shelby with substan-
tially more than a passing interest.

Then everything was business. Once the judge sat
down, Parker grew completely absorbed in the process of jury selection.

So did Shelby, but her absorption included watching the Texan at work. As each potential juror was
brought in for questioning, he smiled charmingly and
greeted them with his slow Texas drawl, instantly
putting them at ease. He asked what appeared to be
inconsequential questions at first and listened politely
to the answers. If a potential juror wandered away
from the point, Parker firmly but patiently brought
him or her back. By the time he'd finished with them,
he knew everything he needed to know about their
background and thought processes, and the juror felt
as though he or she had made a new friend.

This guy is good, she thought.

Then there was Jerry with his quick movements and
brashness, grating on even the most impartial observer as he fired questions supplied to him by Dr.
Carol Hindes. Jerry's naturally abrasive style worked
well in some quarters, but here it didn't contrast well
with Parker's more laid-back approach. Twenty minutes into the process, Shelby could see that, and wondered if he'd notice and tone himself down.

One by one, the jurors were either chosen or re-
jected. By the noon break they had five. By the end of
the day's session, they had twelve and two alternates.

Already she could see that the system here functioned a lot more swiftly than in most other states where it could have taken months to select a jury for a case like this.

When the judge adjourned court for the day, Parker Kincaid leaned over to speak to Jane Mitchell. Then he picked up his stack of files and quickly left the courtroom.

This was a man who had someplace to go.

Shelby put her notebook into her shoulder bag and followed, curious despite herself. The young woman who'd come into court earlier was standing just outside the doors. Parker handed her the stack of files and took a large manila envelope from her, ignoring the reporters as they elbowed their way to him shouting their questions. He said something to the young woman that made her laugh, then headed down the hall past the photographers and cameramen who were barred from the courtroom.

When everyone realized that he wasn't going to stop to give them a statement, they turned their attention to Jerry, whose verbosity more than made up for Parker's silence.

For her part, Shelby was more interested in why Parker was in such a hurry and followed him outside into the late afternoon sun. No sooner had he emerged than a little boy, no more than six and decked out in a baseball uniform with the number four on the chest and back, yelled out "Daddy" and ran into Parker's arms. Parker lifted the boy high into the air, then hugged him and set him on the ground. They both waved to Rosa, who waved back from her station wagon and pulled out of her parking space to drive away.

While Shelby stood on the courthouse steps and watched, Parker and the boy walked to his dusty pickup. He lifted the little boy into the truck, then took off his jacket and tossed it across the back of the seat. His tie joined it a moment later.

Jerry stopped next to her. "Do you believe this heat?" he asked as he took off his jacket and slung it over his shoulder.

She was still watching Parker.

"Shelby?"

"Hmm?"

"I asked if you believed this heat?"

"I've been trying not to think about it."

"A wise woman. What are you going to do now?"

The truck drove away. "Get something cold to drink and then transcribe my notes," she said, turning her attention to Jerry.

"A cold drink sounds terrific. Would you mind if I joined you?" he asked.

"Not at all."

He put his hand under her arm as they went down the remaining few steps. "There's a decent place not too far from here. I happened onto it when I was here for pretrial work." He glanced down at her as they walked. "So, my little critic, what did you think about the jury selection?"

"Quite honestly, it was one of the smoothest and fastest I've ever seen."

He nodded. "Amazing, wasn't it? They don't mess around in Texas."

"I think it also helped that the prosecutor doesn't play silly games in the courtroom."

A corner of his mouth lifted. "Are you saying that I do?"

"You play games in and out of the courtroom, and you know it as well as I do."

"Where I come from, it's called strategy, and I don't apologize for it. It gives the defense a little psychological edge."

"I don't know, Jerry. I think you might have misread the opposition this time."

"You don't think Parker Kincaid is intimidated just a little by my team or the good press we're getting?"

"I don't think he is at all. In fact, I think he finds you amusing."

"Then he's making a big mistake." He pointed to the right. "Here's the place."

They went into a small bar that was so dark Shelby had to wait a minute for her eyes to adjust. She and the defense attorney found a quiet booth and sat down. A man in a white T-shirt walked over to them with a friendly smile. "Can I get you two something?"

"A cold beer," Jerry said. "What about you, Shelby?"

"A glass of iced tea, please."

Jerry studied the woman across from him. "What did you think of my use of Dr. Hindes to help pick the most favorable jury for my client?"

Shelby shook her head. "You don't want to know what I think, Jerry. Trust me. I'll just repeat that I think the simpler you keep things, the more the good people of Dry River Falls will appreciate it."

"I'll let Parker Kincaid keep things simple. I'm going to dazzle them with footwork."

Shelby smiled. "I see. So tell me, Jerry, is your client guilty?"

The attorney wasn't the least bit thrown off guard by her abrupt question. He waited until their drinks had been served before answering. "You think that if you ask me that question enough times, I'll finally blurt out the answer. Well, I'll tell you, Shelby, I don't care if he's guilty or not. I'm not in the business of judging guilt or innocence. I'm here to see that my client gets a fair trial."

Shelby nodded. "I'm not arguing about that. I understand innocent until proven guilty. But the part of being a defense attorney that's always fascinated me is the ability to set aside one's conscience, both social and personal, in pursuit of a specific verdict rather than justice."

"All of my clients have a right to the best defense I can possibly provide them. If police make mistakes in searching for evidence or in not reading someone his rights, it's my job to point that out."

"And what about trying to rig a jury by using a psychologist to tell you how she thinks different jurors will vote?"

He lifted an expressive eyebrow. "Rig? That's pretty strong language, Shelby, even for you."

She lifted her shoulders. "All right. What would you call it, Jerry?"

"I'm just using all the tools I legally can to see that my client gets the fairest shake possible." He studied her closely. The old Shelby that he remembered had been vivacious with sparkling eyes and a mouth that always looked on the verge of smiling. This new Shelby was so subdued. The sparkle was gone. Her smiles now were, at best, half hearted. And yet, to his way of thinking, she was even more beautiful. "You've changed a lot since the last time we saw each other."

"You haven't," she said with a half smile.

"And that's why you love me." He looked at his watch, then reached for his wallet. "I have to get back to the hotel. There's a lot to do before court resumes tomorrow." He put some money on the table and finished his drink. "How about if I pay for the drinks today and you pay next time. Then we can call it even without either of us being beholden to the other."

"All right. Thank you, Jerry. I'll see you in court tomorrow morning."

As soon as he'd gone, Shelby pulled her notebook out of her purse and started writing. People came in and went out. Hours sped by, as they always did when she wrote. One of the most interesting aspects of her work usually had to do with coming into a situation where she knew virtually nothing and following it step-by-step until she had enough knowledge to pull it all together and draw conclusions. This time she knew a little more than she usually did, but not really that much.

She supposed that what she really liked was the way she could get so involved that her work filled her thoughts to the exclusion of all else. It was the only thing that had kept her going for the past year.

She packed up her things and stepped outside. The heat smacked her cool skin like a hot, wet towel. She walked quickly down the narrow sidewalk toward the hotel, anxious to get back to the air conditioning—but not so anxious to get within range of her anonymous telephone caller.

She could handle it.

She could handle anything.

Chapter Four

She walked quickly down the street, oblivious to her surroundings.

"Can I give you a lift somewhere?"

Shelby, startled out of her thoughts, turned to find Parker Kincaid driving slowly beside her in his pickup. He looked hot and sweaty. Shelby kept walking. "I'm just going to the hotel."

"Have you had dinner?"

"Not yet. It's almost too hot to eat."

Parker continued to drive slowly beside her. "My housekeeper can cook her way around the heat. I know she'd like it if you came home with me for dinner."

"Thanks, anyway. I can just grab something at the hotel."

"I know what you can do. I'm simply offering you a more pleasant alternative."

She stopped walking and turned completely and unsmilingly toward him. "Why?"

"Why? That sounds as though you think I have an ulterior motive."

"Do you?"

A corner of his handsome mouth lifted. "Possibly. But I'd be willing to bet it's not the one you think."

Shelby smiled back before she could catch herself.

"So how about dinner? It'll give you a little color commentary on the prosecutor of Dry River Falls for your article."

She started to turn him down, but stopped herself. If this were anyone but Parker Kincaid, she would have jumped at the chance not to return to her hotel room. As it was, she was hesitant, but she accepted, anyway. "All right. Thank you for the invitation."

He reached across the seat and opened the door for her. Shelby climbed gingerly inside.

"Not what you're used to, I imagine," he said of his pickup truck. His tone was without apology.

"Not quite."

Parker swung the truck around and drove for just over one block before parking in front of an old-fashioned ice cream parlor. The little boy she'd seen earlier came running out with an ice cream cone that had already started to melt. Parker got out and lifted the boy onto the seat so that he was sitting between the two adults. Then Parker climbed into the driver's seat. "I'll hold your cone while you put on your seat belt."

The little boy handed him the cone and licked his fingers before reaching for his seatbelt.

Parker looked at Shelby over the boy's dark head. "Shelby, I'd like you to meet my son, Danny. Danny, this is Mrs. Chassen."

Danny smiled at her. Two perfect dimples creased his rounded cheeks. "Hi."

She smiled back. It was impossible not to. "Hi. How'd your ball game go?"

He wrinkled his nose. "We lost. Fifty-one to forty-six." He spoke with just the tiniest lisp.

Shelby had to bite the inside of her cheek to keep from smiling. "I'm sorry."

He nodded as he took back the cone from his father. "We've lost three games in a row now," he said unhappily. "Some of the kids don't mind losing, but this is my career we're talking about."

She looked at Parker, her eyes brimming with laughter.

"Danny wants to be a baseball player when he grows up," he said, returning her look with smiling eyes of his own.

"Do you like baseball?" Danny asked her.

"I played on a team when I was your age."

He looked at her with a new respect. "Were you any good?"

"I was brilliant. My grandmother said so."

"Wow! What are your statistics?"

"Oh, dear. It was a long time ago, Danny. I'm afraid I don't remember."

He nodded. "That's all right. Rosa says that when you get old the first thing to go is your mind."

"Danny!" Parker said as he took the main road out of town and headed into the countryside.

"How old are you?" Danny asked her ingenuously, looking at her sideways as he turned his cone around to lick the drippy side.

"Twenty-five," she said before Parker could utter the protest on his lips. "How old are you?"

"I'm six years and three months old."

"You look like you're seven," she said seriously.

Danny beamed at her. "You're all right for a girl."

"Thank you, Danny. That's the nicest compliment I've had in a long time."

Parker turned onto the rutted gravel and dirt road that led to his house. The tires kicked up a thick wall of dust that trailed after them the entire way. Shelby had to hold on to the dashboard to keep from being thrown all over the inside of the truck as it bounced its way over the ruts.

She gazed through the passenger window at the land. It was vast and brown and gold. It looked thirsty.

Parker guessed her thoughts. "I know it doesn't seem like much right now, but you should have seen it when we first moved here. We've made a lot of progress."

"What do you raise?"

"Cattle mostly. Over the next few years, as I get the pastures fenced in and some proper irrigation, I hope to gradually increase the size of my herd."

"I have my own horse," Danny told her. "And a dog."

The narrow road suddenly opened up and there was the house. Here, everything was well-tended, right down to the fresh coat of white paint on the house. A bench swing hung from the rafters of the porch.

"This is lovely," she said as he parked the truck at the side of the house. "I couldn't really see it last night."

"When I bought this place, no one had lived here for twenty years. It took me quite a while just to make it habitable." Parker got out of the truck and lifted Danny to the ground. "Go tell Rosa we're going to have a guest for dinner and then wash your hands and face."

As the little boy ran off, Parker walked around the truck to Shelby's side. She'd already opened her door and was getting ready to step out when Parker's strong hands caught her waist and lifted her to the ground.

With her hands resting on his upper arms, Shelby looked up at him in surprise. "Thank you."

His eyes moved over her heat-flushed face. "You're welcome."

Shelby lowered her own eyes and stepped away from the man, deeply uncomfortable with his nearness and remembering all too clearly how his lips had felt on hers last night.

Parker didn't say anything as he reached past her to the dashboard to pick up the manila envelope she'd seen his secretary give him earlier at the courthouse. His long body brushed against hers. Shelby moved back as far as she could until her back was pressed against the doorjamb. Parker got the envelope, then leaned away from Shelby and looked down at her. "I don't bite," he said quietly.

"I know. I just don't like to be touched."

"By anyone or just by me?"

She didn't answer, but her look didn't waiver.

The screen door on the veranda opened with a creak and slammed shut. "Parker?" called a woman's voice.

"Over here, Rosa."

The housekeeper walked to the edge of the veranda and leaned over the railing. Her round body was wrapped in an apron. "Danny said you brought home company for dinner." She beamed as soon as she caught sight of Shelby. "Hello! How's your ankle feeling?"

"Much better, thank you."

Despite what Shelby had just said about not liking to be touched, Parker put his hand under her arm and guided her to the veranda. She drew her arm away and spoke to Rosa. "I hope that my coming here so unexpectedly isn't a problem."

"Oh, no, no. I always make plenty of food."

Parker and Shelby walked around to the steps and up to the porch. "If you don't mind," he said, "I'm going to take a quick shower before dinner. Rosa can keep you company."

The housekeeper looped her arm through Shelby's and walked her into the house while Parker disappeared up the stairs. "Come talk to me while I work."

"Is there anything I can help you with?" Shelby asked as they went into the kitchen.

"No, thank you. I have only a few things left to do." Rosa waved toward a stool set behind the counter.

"How long have you worked here?" Shelby asked as she sat down.

"Five years—ever since Parker and Danny moved to Dry River Falls."

Danny, all cleaned up now, came walking in with a fuzzy white puppy trailing in his footsteps. "I'm really hungry, Rosa. When's dinner?"

"As soon as your father finishes his shower, we'll set out the food."

He grabbed a slice of bread from a basket on the counter. "Bear and I are going outside to play."

"All right. Just don't get all dirty again."

The kitchen door slammed after him as he and the puppy ran outside.

Shelby's eyes, a tender look in their depths, followed him. "He's a wonderful little boy."

Rosa smiled. "He really is, though sometimes he seems like a man in a little boy's body. He's very serious. And his mind..." She shook her head. "He reads so much and never forgets anything." As Rosa tore lettuce into a large bowl, she studied the younger woman. "How are you enjoying your stay in Dry River Falls?"

"It's a little hot for my taste, but I imagine I'll get used to it eventually." She watched Rosa as she worked. "Do you know anything about the trial that Parker's involved in?"

"Only what I read in the papers. He never talks about his work. I know J. W. Lyle, of course, and I knew his wife. Everyone knows everyone here."

"What did you think of them as a couple?"

She shrugged her large shoulders. "They seemed happy enough. She was a lovely woman, and he seemed like a nice enough fellow."

"So you don't think he killed his wife?"

"I don't know. No one really does except J.W."

The phone rang. Rosa wiped her hands on her apron as she crossed the room to the wall phone. "Kincaid residence."

She listened. "One moment, dear. I'll get him." She laid the phone on the counter, then she left the kitchen and went to the staircase. "Telephone for you, Parker," she called out. "It's your secretary. You'll have to take it in the kitchen. The phone in your study is still broken."

A minute later he strolled into the kitchen. His hair was wet, and he was carrying his shirt in his hand. "Yeah," he said, cradling the phone between his head and his shoulder as he put on his shirt.

Against her will, Shelby's eyes were drawn to him. His skin was tanned from working in the hot Texas sun. His shoulders were broad and straight; the muscles in his back and arms were smooth and well-defined. He turned slightly as he switched the phone to the other ear and she saw the solid wall of his flat stomach. Her eyes moved slowly up over his chest, following the path of his fingers as he buttoned his shirt from the bottom up. When she got to his face, he was looking straight at her, obviously amused by her scrutiny.

Shelby could feel her cheeks flush, but she wouldn't let him intimidate her into looking away like she was a little girl caught doing something she shouldn't. Instead, she waited until he picked up a pencil and started to write on a notepad before she rose and walked outside onto the porch. Leaning forward with her hands clenching the railing, she took a deep breath and slowly exhaled, letting the evening air relax her. She stayed there for a minute or two, then straightened and followed the porch around to the front of the house and sat on the bench swing.

It was dusk. The air was beginning to cool off. There was even a slight breeze that lifted Shelby's damp hair away from her neck. Danny was in the yard throwing a stick for the puppy to fetch. Unfortunately, the puppy hadn't quite figured out what he was supposed to do with the stick. He raced after it on his short little legs and then stood over it yipping.

Danny walked over to the puppy, shaking his head. "No, Bear. You're not supposed to bark at it. You're supposed to pick it up and bring it to me. Then I throw it again and you chase it and bring it back to me." Danny thought about what he'd said for a second, then laughed and hugged the puppy. "No wonder you don't want to do it. It's a pretty dumb game, and you have to do all the work."

Shelby tilted her head to one side. A soft smile touched her lips as she watched the boy and the puppy rolling on the ground together.

Parker came outside and stood leaning against the railing, facing his son. His eyes, however, were on Shelby. As soon as she realized it, her smile faded.

"Don't do that, Shelby."

Her eyes met his. "Do what?"

"As soon as you notice someone watching you, it's as though you pull yourself into a shell."

"I didn't realize."

"Why do you suppose you do that?"

She lifted her shoulders in a delicate shrug. "Perhaps because a shell is such a safe place to be."

"And being safe is important to you?"

She looked at him for a long moment before answering. "It's the most important thing of all."

"What if I were to say to you that the world is a wonderful place and you have nothing to fear from it? You don't need to hide yourself away."

"I'd say that you don't know me well enough to know what I fear."

"I know you better than you think I do."

Shelby gave him a look that had "poor deluded man" written all over it.

"For instance," Parker said, taking up her unspoken challenge, "you're afraid of me."

"Now, why would I be afraid of you?" she asked evenly.

He walked over to her, towering over her, and raised her face to his. "You're afraid because I make you feel things that you don't think you're ready to feel yet." He trailed his fingers over the fine line of her jaw and down her throat, coming to rest at the vulnerable spot at its base. "You say you don't like to be touched, but the problem is that you do like it when I touch you, Shelby." He moved his fingertips gently within the circle of that soft spot and then grew still. "Your pulse is racing right now. I can feel it. You can, too."

Shelby looked into his eyes, mesmerized. She wanted to get away from him; away from his husky, deep voice. But she couldn't.

He bent at the knee so that they were eye level. Taking her hand in his, he placed it on his chest, over the spot where his heart was, and held it there. She could feel its strong, steady beat through her fingertips. It echoed through her body. "You enjoyed the kiss we shared last night as much as I did." He leaned closer to her as he separated her fingers against his chest with a single slow stroke of his own fingers and twined them together, still holding her hand against his heart. "Last night as you lay alone in your bed, you wondered what it would feel like if you could shed all of your inhibitions—all of your guilt about being with another man—and just let yourself go with me. You wondered what it would be like if I kissed you here." He trailed his finger to her earlobe. "And here." He moved his hand under her hair and around to the back of her neck. "And here." Shelby closed her eyes as his fingers found their way down her throat and over the soft swell of her breast. "I know that's what you thought about last night, Shelby, because I had the same thoughts."

Shelby opened her eyes and looked into his.

Parker sighed as he cupped her cheek in the palm of his hand. "I want to know you better. I want you to know me. I'd like to take things slowly because I know you feel you need the time, but in a matter of weeks this trial will be over and you'll be gone. I don't want to spend the rest of my life wondering if letting you go was a mistake.''

Parker's words took Shelby completely by surprise. Her confusion showed in her tawny eyes.

A corner of his mouth lifted, deepening the groove in his cheek. ''Honey,'' he said in that drawl, ''I know that you're afraid of getting hurt, and you have no reason to trust me. But don't shut me out because of what happened to your husband. I know you miss him. I can see it in your eyes. But he's gone and I'm here. Give me a chance. Give yourself a chance.'' He moved his hand around to the back of her head and began to draw her toward him.

Shelby's breath caught in her throat.

''Danny!'' Rosa called out. ''Wash your hands again and help me carry dinner out. We're eating on the porch.''

Shelby was so startled that she jumped. She'd forgotten about everyone but Parker.

''Okay! Come on, Bear.'' Boy and puppy ran around to the side of the house. There was the clop-clop of sneakered feet as they ran up the steps and the slam of the screen door.

The spell was broken and Parker knew it. His hand fell to his side but his gaze never wavered. Without saying anything further, he rose and walked back to the railing just as Rosa came around the corner of the porch with a tray holding plates, glasses and a large salad bowl. While Shelby watched him, Parker took it from his housekeeper and set it on a round white table.

"This is a nice, cool dinner for a warm evening," Rosa said as she put some salad onto a plate and handed it to Shelby.

Shelby smiled absently. "Thank you."

Danny gave her silverware and a napkin. Parker poured her a glass of iced tea and held it toward her. When Shelby reached for it, her fingers touched his.

The muscle in his cheek tightened and relaxed. He let go of the glass. Shelby could breathe again.

Rosa didn't miss any of this byplay as she served everyone, then sat on the swing beside Shelby. "This is sort of my version of a Mexican chef's salad," she said. "A little spicy meat, some cheese, tomato, avocado and my own special dressing."

Parker and Danny sat on the top step of the veranda talking about baseball. It was friendly and peaceful, just the way Shelby imagined ordinary family life to be.

Rosa looked at her and smiled. "You have an interesting expression on your face. What are you thinking?"

Shelby took a sip of her iced tea. "How different this is from my own home when I was a child."

"Different in what way?" Parker asked, suddenly turning his attention to her.

"My parents were very formal people who insisted on perfect manners at all times, whatever the circumstances."

"Even when it was just you and your family?" Danny asked.

"Even then."

Rosa inclined her head toward Shelby's left hand. "Well, now you have your own family so you can behave any way you wish."

Shelby looked at the ring as well.

Parker saw Shelby's downcast face, and a sudden and very unaccustomed protectiveness welled in him. "Rosa, would you like some more iced tea?" he asked to change the subject.

She looked at him curiously. He could see perfectly that her glass was nearly full. "No, thank you."

Shelby turned to Rosa and pointed toward the salad with her fork. "This is delicious."

"Thank you, dear. Do you enjoy cooking?"

"Very much, when I have the time."

"The beauty of this salad, of course, is that it doesn't take much time at all. Next time you visit, I'll show you just how simple it is to make."

"I'd like that."

"The salad, of course, is easy. It's the sauce that's a little tricky."

Danny's fork clanked onto his plate. "I'm all finished. Can I go watch TV?"

"May I," Parker corrected him. "And yes, you may. Take your plate to the kitchen and rinse it off."

"Okay." He ran around the porch to the kitchen door. They heard the fork clatter to the floor, a moment of silence, the fork being tossed onto the plate and then the slamming of the screen door.

Parker set his plate on the porch and leaned back against the railing, his eyes on Shelby.

Rosa looked from one to the other, then reached for Shelby's plate. "I think I'll just take these inside."

"Oh, here," Shelby said as she started to rise, not wanting to be left alone with Parker, "let me help you."

Rosa put her hand on Shelby's shoulder and pressed her back onto the swing. "You're not allowed to help until at least the third visit. Besides, there's very little to do. That's the other nice thing about this kind of dinner." She stacked Parker's plate on the other two and disappeared around the corner and into the kitchen.

Parker was still looking at Shelby, and she was intensely aware of it. She raised her wrist to study her watch. "I suppose I should be getting back to the hotel."

"Were you in love with your husband?" Parker asked.

Her eyes swung to the man sitting about eight feet away, leaning against the porch railing. The only light came from a window behind them. "I think that's a rather personal question."

"I know. Were you?"

Shelby looked into the darkness. "I loved Eric."

"But were you *in* love with him?"

"The relationship we had is difficult to explain. We grew up together. We went to the same schools, joined the same clubs, enjoyed the same things." She smiled softly. "We could talk about anything. He was always there for me, and I was always there for him. I married my best friend." She grew thoughtful. "And a year ago I buried him." Shelby suddenly got to her feet. "I'd like to go back to the hotel now."

Parker rose also. He somehow knew without being told that this was the first time she'd talked about her husband like that since his death. He gently caught her hand in his and walked her down the steps and around the house to his truck. After he helped her into the pickup, Shelby followed him with her eyes as he walked around the front of the vehicle and climbed into the driver's side. His gentleness had caught her offguard.

Parker started the engine and turned on the headlights, illuminating the gravel road that cut through his property. Then he pushed a cassette into the tape deck and a Rachmaninoff piano concerto in all of its richness filled the silence as he put the truck into gear and started driving.

Shelby glanced at him in surprise. A tape of Rachmaninoff was the last thing she'd expected Parker to play.

Parker turned his head and flashed his lazy smile. "That's right, princess, even cowboys can appreciate classical music." He changed gears, and the truck sped ahead, sending gravel flying out from under the rear tires.

Shelby stared through the windshield. The wind coming through her open window whipped her hair in all directions, but she didn't mind. It felt good. Cleansing. She closed her eyes and turned her face fully into it.

It seemed like only a few minutes later that Parker pulled to a stop in front of her hotel. Shelby reluctantly opened her eyes and turned to Parker. "Thank you for dinner."

"You're not getting rid of me that easily." He shut off the engine and got out of the truck to open the door for her.

"There's no need to walk me to my room."

He put his hands at her waist and lifted her to the ground. "There's every need," he said softly. "Have you gotten any more calls since last night?"

She shook her head.

"Good. While the trial was going on today, my secretary had the police and telephone records regarding your sick friend faxed to my office."

"Why?" Shelby asked, bemused.

"Because, despite my best efforts not to be, I'm worried about you. I've also arranged for your hotel phone to be tapped starting tomorrow." He looked at her closely with a hint of a smile. "You're not mad at me, are you?"

It was hard not to smile back. The man could be completely charming. "I'm not mad, exactly. I guess I'm just used to taking care of myself."

"So I've noticed."

Together they went into the hotel and, in silence took the elevator to her floor.

She opened her door and flicked on the light. Parker walked past her and checked out the entire suite, closets and all. All was well.

When he went back into the hall where Shelby waited by the door, he looked down at her. "I don't suppose you want to invite me in for a nightcap," he said.

She shook her head. "No. Thanks again for dinner. And please thank Rosa for me."

"You can thank her yourself next time."

"There probably won't be a next time."

"Why not?"

"Parker, I can't get involved with you. I think it's best if I just stay around here and do my work."

His eyes moved over her lovely face. "Whether you know it or not, you're already involved with me." He touched his finger to her lips. "Good night, Shelby."

"Good night."

He stood still for a moment, looking at her, then turned away and walked to the stairs.

Shelby stayed where she was until he'd disappeared. She closed the door, then leaned her back against it. He was a wonderful man, and he was right. She was very attracted to him.

But she didn't want to be.

She twisted her gold wedding band with the fingers of her right hand. She'd been numb ever since Eric's death. She welcomed that numbness. She embraced it and held on to it like a protective blanket for her emotions. It was the only way she'd been able to function for the past twelve months.

What Shelby didn't welcome was the awakening of her senses that seemed to happen whenever she was around Parker Kincaid. She was genuinely afraid of him. Afraid of what she knew she could feel when she was with him if she let herself.

The phone rang.

Shelby knew who it was going to be even before she answered it, but she answered it anyway.

"You betrayed me," the voice whispered harshly. "You betrayed me just like she did."

"Betrayed you? How? What are you talking about?"

There was only the sound of the wind.

Parker walked from his truck to the front of his house and climbed up the steps to the porch. Rosa was sitting on the swing seat, rocking gently back and forth. "You left rather suddenly," she said.

"You could say that."

"She's a beautiful woman."

"Yes," he agreed, "she is."

"But?" Rosa asked.

He sat on the top step and looked out at the night. "She lost her husband, and she hasn't gotten over it. I don't know if she ever will."

"Perhaps you can help her."

Parker shook his head. "I'm not so sure, Rosa."

She continued to swing back and forth. "It's a terrible thing to lose a husband at so young an age."

Parker nodded.

"It takes some people longer than others to recover from emotional blows like that."

"And some people never recover. They let their silent grief eat away at them until there's nothing left but an empty shell of a human being."

"Parker," Rosa said as she stopped the swing, "if you feel something for this woman, don't let her shut you out. Make her confront her feelings. Help her get out of this prison she's built for herself."

"Oh, Rosa," he said as he tiredly rubbed his eyes, "this whole thing is crazy. I've just met the woman. I don't understand why she matters to me. She's not even my type."

Rosa smiled.

Parker glanced at her out of the corner of his eye. "What's so amusing?"

"In all of the years I've know you, I've never seen you look at a woman that way you looked at Shelby Chassen tonight."

"You said it yourself. She's beautiful."

"That's not it and you know it. There was a tenderness in your eyes. I think, Parker, that you're in some danger of falling in love with the woman, if you haven't already."

Parker stood up, walked over to Rosa and kissed her cheek. "I've never really been in love in my life, and if I were going to start now, I certainly wouldn't chose a wounded bird whose heart clearly belongs to another man. There are times, my dear Rosa, when you don't know me as well as you think."

"And there are other times when I know you better than you know yourself."

Parker just smiled. "Is Danny in bed?"

"I just tucked him in a few minutes ago. I told him the puppy could sleep with him tonight. Is that all right with you?"

"Sure. I think I'll go say good-night and then I'm going to have to go back to my office and do some work."

"At this hour?"

"Jury selection is over. The hard part starts tomorrow. I have a few things I need to do before then."

"Want me to make you a thermos of coffee?"

"I'd appreciate it." He disappeared into the house.

Rosa pushed against the veranda floor with her foot and set the swing in motion, her dark eyes thoughtful.

Chapter Five

For the next several days, Shelby attended court, took her notes, had dinner alone and worked in her room until the early morning hours. It was beginning to look as though the trial was going to end more quickly than anyone had imagined.

There had been no more phone calls, but the last one had been enough to keep her looking over her shoulder.

She'd avoided Parker by packing up her things as soon as court ended and escaping through the throngs of reporters that crowded around him shouting questions and taking pictures.

But there was no avoiding watching him in the courtroom. The more she watched and listened, the more her respect for the man grew. He was straightforward and polite with everyone. There was neither theatrics nor trickery. Day by day he steadily built his case against the defendant and gently pulled the jury right along with him.

And Shelby.

He'd built a sympathetic portrait of Diane Lyle as a career woman who thought she'd found her Prince Charming—and perhaps for a time she had. But her prince had a temper, and Diane was in the wrong place at the wrong time when that temper erupted one night. As he moved through the evidence, circumstantial as it might have been, and questioned the experts who interpreted that evidence, it was clear that Parker had done his scientific homework. He knew exactly what questions to ask. Despite Jerry's constant and frequently annoying objections and his manner of hammering away at the prosecution witnesses on cross-examination, Parker never once responded in kind. He was like the calm in the center of a storm.

On this particular morning, Shelby looked around the steaming courtroom for Charles Greene, the photographer the magazine had sent to Texas just yesterday, as she fanned her face with her notebook. As always, she'd arrived early to ensure getting a good seat.

A court clerk came in and set up two large freestanding fans to help stir the air. Their great faces turned slowly back and forth. Shelby relished those few seconds with each turn that the fans blew on her and unconsciously fell into her own rhythm with them. Over the next several hours, she came to expect the small bursts of air on her hot skin.

Every day there was the same routine of the defendant and his team of attorneys and assistants filing in. Today was no different. J.W. turned in his seat and winked at Shelby. She inclined her head in acknowledgement, but didn't smile.

When she heard Parker's gravelly voice in the back of the courtroom, her heart caught—just as it always did when he was nearby. The defendant heard it, too, and his smoothly handsome face filled with a hatred so deep it was frightening to behold. Jerry said something to his client and the moment passed, but it was a memory that stayed with Shelby for the rest of the trial. And it gave her her first dark glimpse at the man behind J. W. Lyle's bland, flirtatious exterior.

Could the whisperer be like that? Bland one moment and full of hatred the next?

The photographer came into the room and sat next to Shelby in the chair she'd been saving for him. "Here," he said, handing her a cup with coffee in it. "Anything going on?" he asked.

"Thanks, Charles. Not yet."

"I got some great shots of Lyles's house. He's got a lot of security, though, so I couldn't get anything through the windows. Couldn't get close enough."

"Maybe there's something in the police files that's usable."

"Good idea. I'll check on it. I just need a few more shots of the town and I can call it a wrap."

"Did you get some of Lyle's sister?" She pointed out a tall woman sitting directly behind Lyle.

"Sure did."

UP TO 6 FREE GIFTS FOR YOU!
Look inside—all gifts are absolutely free!

NO POSTAGE
NECESSARY
IF MAILED
IN THE
UNITED STATES

BUSINESS REPLY MAIL
FIRST CLASS MAIL   PERMIT NO. 717   BUFFALO, NY

POSTAGE WILL BE PAID BY ADDRESSEE

SILHOUETTE READER SERVICE
3010 WALDEN AVE
PO BOX 1867
BUFFALO NY 14240-9952

Behind These Doors!

GIFTS

"It's a shame they won't let you take pictures inside the courtroom. I'd love to have a candid photo of Lyle's reaction to the verdict when it comes in."

"What do you think it's going to be?"

"Guilty. Unless Jerry has some rabbits he can pull out of his hat, he's been out-lawyered by the prosecutor."

"That Kincaid guy's pretty good, is he?"

"Very."

"Yeah, well, I'd better be going. The light's real good right now."

She looked at Charles and smiled. He was a nice man, perhaps twenty years older than Shelby. "When are you planning to leave for New York?"

"Tomorrow afternoon. I'll send you prints of what I have. You and your editor can pick through them to see what's appropriate for the article."

"Thanks."

"Do you want to have dinner with me tonight?" he asked.

"Thanks, Charles, but I don't think so. I'm just going to have a sandwich in my room and write."

"Sure. Okay. I'll talk to you whenever, then."

"It was nice working with you again, Charles."

He smiled at her. "I enjoyed it, too. Maybe we can do it again sometime."

Parker passed Charles in the aisle as he walked to the prosecutor's table and sat down. A moment later the jury and judge entered.

Despite her best efforts, Shelby's eyes were drawn to him. He took off his jacket and hung it over the back of his chair. Then he rolled the sleeves of his

blue-striped white shirt halfway up his strong fore-
arms. He seemed oblivious to the other people in the
courtroom as he pulled his legal pad toward him and
began to jot down some notes.

He called his witness. He half leaned, half sat on the
edge of the prosecution's table as he asked his questions. Shelby watched him, noting every time he
pushed his fingers through his hair, every time he
moved his arms, stretching the cloth of his shirt tightly
across his broad shoulders. At one point while listening to his witness, Parker twisted his upper body
around to pick up a document from the table. He
seemed to know exactly where Shelby was because he
looked straight into her eyes and kept looking at her.
As soon as the witness had finished speaking, Parker,
without missing a beat, straightened, turned around
and asked his next question.

Shelby looked down at her notepad and started
writing, but her mind was on Parker Kincaid. It
seemed as though her mind was always on Parker
lately.

To everyone's surprise, Parker rested his case.

Then it was Jerry's turn. The first witness he called
was his own client. J.W. took the stand trying to look
sober and sad, but could not quite pull it off. His
cockiness was there, peeking through the facade.

Jerry took him step-by-step through his first meeting with Diane, their courtship and their marriage.
When Jerry had him describe the night his wife was
killed, J.W. even managed to cry.

Shelby realized as she watched that she didn't believe any of it. Parker had convinced her with his evi-

dence, and if this was the best Jerry could offer—well, it wasn't good enough for her and she didn't think it was going to be good enough for a jury.

The judge suddenly interrupted the proceedings to recess court for a late lunch. Shelby quickly packed her shoulder bag.

"Have lunch with me, Shelby."

She looked up to find Parker standing over her.

"Lunch?" she said blankly.

"Surprised that I caught you before you could run away this time?" he asked, obviously amused.

Shelby didn't say anything.

"We both have to eat so we might as well do it together."

She still didn't say anything.

Parker tried again, leaning closer to her. "You can't avoid me forever, you know."

Shelby could have said no, but she didn't. With the way the trial was going, she knew she'd be gone soon. "All right."

His mouth curved in a slow, approving smile. "I have to drop off my files first."

Together they took the stairs to his office on the third floor. It was small and neat. His secretary looked up from her computer with a smile. "How'd it go?"

He shrugged. "Ask me again in a week. Anything going on that I need to take care of?"

"Just a few phone calls. Nothing really urgent." She was paying more attention to Shelby than to Parker.

He put the files on the corner of her desk. "Bring these back down to the courtroom around one-thirty. Mrs. Chassen and I are going out for lunch."

The secretary smiled knowingly at Shelby. Shelby wondered exactly what it was the woman knew as she smiled back at her.

As they walked down the street, Parker took Shelby's elbow and felt her stiffen. As he glanced down at her, his mouth curved into a slow smile. "Have you asked yourself why it is that I make you so uneasy?"

She looked up at him. "No, but you've apparently asked yourself that question. What answer did you come up with?"

"Don't be coy, Shelby. It doesn't become you."

"I'm curious, not coy."

"You want me," he said with a devilish glint in his eye as he opened the door to an air-conditioned bar named Jake's and held it for her.

Her mouth formed a perfect O. "I what?"

"Want, not what. Deny it."

"I deny it. Categorically."

He pressed his hand against the center of her back and guided her to a booth near a window.

A tall barrel of a man wearing a white half apron walked over to them and slapped Parker on the shoulder. "Hey, counselor. How's that boy of yours?"

"Danny's just fine, Jake, except for losing another ball game last night."

"Lost again, did he?" He shook his large white head. "What that team needs is a new coach."

"I'm the coach."

"I rest my case."

Parker laughed as he looked at Shelby. "Jake thinks the occasional spitball is the answer. Shelby Chassen, this is Jake Crandal, the owner."

Jake took her hand into his great paw and gave it a vigorous shake. "Pleased to meet you."

"Hello, Jake." She liked him instantly.

"Shelby's covering the Lyle trial for a magazine," Parker explained.

"Is that so? I could tell you stories about that boy. Why I remember the time..."

"Jake," Parker interrupted, "we'd both love to hear your stories, but we don't have a lot of time right now. We have to be back in court in less than an hour."

"I'd like to talk to you when we have more time," Shelby said.

"You just come in anytime, little lady. I'm always here. Now, what would you two like to eat?"

"May I have a menu, please?" Shelby asked.

"No menu. Don't need one. You have a choice of a hamburger with fries, steak sandwich with fries or a chicken sandwich with fries."

"I think I'll have the steak sandwich," Parker said. "What about you, Shelby?"

"That sounds good. I'll have that, too."

"I'll get those right out to you. Anything to drink?"

"Iced tea, please," Shelby said.

"Water for me." Parker looked at her as Jake walked away. "Jake is one of the more colorful characters in town, but he's a good old man. His family's been here in Dry River Falls for nearly five generations."

"He must know everyone."

"Some better than others. He has very definite opinions on everyone. You'd be wise to check out whatever information he gives you."

She gazed at the man across from her. "How do you feel about the case you've presented to the jury?"

"If a vote was taken today, Lyle would be on his way to prison by nightfall." He leaned casually back in his chair. "You were there. How do you think it went?"

"Your evidence was mostly circumstantial, but very convincing. Of course, Jerry hasn't finished putting on his defense yet."

"And I'm sure he'll be very imaginative."

"That's why he wins all of his cases."

"Not this time."

"Do you always win?" Shelby asked.

He leveled his eyes at her. "Always, Shelby."

Jake, balancing two plates in one large hand and glasses of water and iced tea and a bottle of catsup in the other, set their food on the table. "If you two want anything else, just give a yell."

"Thanks, Jake." Parker looked down at his plate. "I can almost hear my arteries clogging."

"Hey, if you want pine nuts, go back to Houston," Jake said gruffly. "Here, we eat real food." Then he winked at Shelby and went back to the bar.

"I think Jake likes you," Parker said as he popped a fry into his mouth.

"How can you tell?"

"He's less abrasive with you than he is with most people."

Shelby laughed, and once again Parker found that the sound delighted him.

They ate in silence for a time, each lost in their own thoughts. Shelby looked at Parker as a prelude to saying something, but his expression stopped her. After all the earlier banter, he looked really troubled. "What's wrong?"

He looked up, startled out of his reverie. "Why do you ask that?"

"Because something obviously is."

He didn't say anything for a moment. "Can we talk about this case off the record?"

"Of course."

"My head tells me that J.W. killed Diane. The evidence is all there."

"But?"

"But my instincts tell me that he didn't do it."

Shelby's eyes widened. "Then why are you prosecuting him?"

"I already told you, the evidence all points to his guilt. I represent the state. It's not up to me to either prosecute or not prosecute a person based on my instincts, but on the facts of the case. And the facts of this case say he did it."

"What are you going to do? You've obviously all but won the case."

"I've had an investigator on this since the first day. He hasn't been able to come up with anything. J.W. hasn't been any help. From day one he was arrogant and combative and wouldn't talk to anyone without his lawyer. Jerry's had his own investigator working around the clock, but as far as I know, he hasn't come up with anything, either. If he had, he would have brought it up in court by now."

"Have you told Jerry about your doubts?"

"Yes. At the very beginning of the case. I wanted to know if he'd found anything that could be used in proving J.W.'s innocence. Jerry just thought I was pumping him for information that I could use to build my own case."

"I'm afraid Jerry's a little cynical. Where he comes from, the attorneys play to win."

"So do I, but I also want to be able to look at myself in the mirror."

"Has J.W. taken a lie detector test?"

"Privately. Jerry won't tell me the results, which means that they were probably inconclusive or J.W. just flat-out failed."

"Do you think he'd fail even if he were innocent?"

"It happens. Maybe he once wished his wife dead when he was mad at her and that's what came out on the test. Who knows?"

Shelby's gaze moved over his handsome face. "You're a surprising man."

He looked at her inquiringly.

"You have a conscience."

"Are you implying that most men don't?"

"I don't know most men."

"I think we've had this conversation before."

"A similar one." Shelby smiled at him. Really smiled. It took his breath away.

Shelby looked at her watch. "I'm going to have to leave. I want to stop at the hotel before I go back to court." She opened her purse and took out some money. "I'm not sure how much the bill is," she said as she put it on the table next to her plate, "but this should cover my portion."

"You won't even let me buy your lunch?"

"It doesn't look good."

"Ah."

Shouldering her bag, she rose from her chair. "I'll see you in court."

Parker didn't say anything. He just watched her walk away from him.

When Shelby got back to the hotel, she tossed her purse onto the bed then stepped into her bathroom and splashed some cool water onto her hot face. She let some of it trickle down her throat and between her breasts, then dabbed at herself with a towel.

As she tossed the towel onto the counter, she caught sight of her reflection in the mirror above the sink. Her cheeks actually had some color in them. Her eyes were alive. It was a portrait of the way she used to be.

Shelby lowered her eyes, unable to stand the sight of herself. How could she even think of being happy? It wasn't right.

Walking back into the bedroom, she sank onto the edge of the bed and lay back, staring at the ceiling.

The telephone rang.

Shelby turned her head and looked at it.

It rang again.

Taking a deep breath, she rolled onto her stomach and picked up the receiver. "Hello?"

"Hello, stranger!"

Shelby smiled with relief. "Katy! How wonderful to hear your voice."

"How's it going?"

"All right. The trial should be over soon. A lot sooner that I expected."

"Are you coming back to Vermont?"

"I'll probably stop off in New York first, but I should be back there in ten days or so."

There was a pause. "You sound odd. Are you sure everything's all right?"

Katy knew her far too well. "Everything's fine. I'll talk to you when I see you."

"You'll talk to me now. What's going on?"

Shelby rolled onto her back and stared at the ceiling. "Nothing, really."

"Oh! It's a man!" Katy said happily. "Come on, tell me! What's his name?"

"Katy, you're incorrigible."

"I know. What's his name?"

"Really, there's no one."

"All right, there's no one. Just tell me who the most interesting man in town is?"

"That's something I can answer. Parker Kincaid. He's the prosecuting attorney in this trial."

"What's he like?"

Shelby smiled. "He's difficult to describe. Suffice to say that he's nothing like Eric."

"Is that a problem?"

"What do you mean?"

"Does he have to be like Eric?"

"Well, no, that's not what I meant. It doesn't matter who he's like. I'm not interested in him in that way."

"I see." Katy didn't believe a word of it.

"What do you mean, you see?"

"Oh, nothing. Just 'I see.' Is he nice?"

"Very."

"Do you like him?"

"Like seems a very mild word in describing anyone's feelings toward him. He's much more vivid than that."

Shelby glanced at the clock by the side of her bed and abruptly sat up. "Oh, Katy, I have to go. I'm going to be late for court."

"Call me soon, okay?"

"I will."

"And say hello for me to your Parker Kincaid."

"He's not mine."

"Right."

As soon as Shelby hung up, she raced to her bathroom to put on some lipstick. Her favorite wasn't there. She looked all over the counter, but it was gone. It had been there that morning because she'd used it. She went back to the bedroom and upended her shoulder bag. It wasn't there, either. Shelby shook her head as she put everything back in. She'd been continuously misplacing things lately. It wasn't like her at all.

Skipping the lipstick, she ran out of her room, slammed the door behind her, and made her way to the courthouse without slackening her pace. The trial was already underway. She looked all over for a seat, finally spotting a narrow bench space next to a local spectator. Shelby squeezed in beside her, apologizing quietly. The woman did her best to give Shelby a little extra space, but it was definitely tight.

Her eyes went straight to Parker. He'd angled his chair so that he was facing the defense table and the witness stand. He seemed completely relaxed with his long legs stretched out in front of him. And his attention was completely focused on the proceedings.

For her part, Shelby listened to J.W. attempt to recount how close he and his wife were. He wasn't very convincing. Once again it was his arrogance that got in the way.

Shelby looked at Parker for his reaction, but his expression was impassive and gave no hint of his thoughts.

Jerry really tried to make J.W. look like a regular guy, but it just wasn't coming together. He tried to portray him as Mr. Everyman, who happened to have a little money and who loved his wife. There was a hollow ring to it. Shelby, as the afternoon progressed, grew convinced that J.W. hadn't been in love with Diane when she was killed. That didn't mean he killed her, of course, but it added yet another sad element to the whole affair. Listening to J.W. talk made his and Diane's life sound so empty and pathetic.

She was relieved when court finally adjourned for the weekend. As she was putting her notebook into her shoulder bag, Jerry walked back to her. "J.W. says he wants to talk to you."

She looked at him in surprise. "I thought he was against it unless I met his conditions?"

"Not any longer."

"What changed his mind?"

Jerry shrugged. "Don't quote me, but I can't begin to get inside the guy's head."

"You sound frustrated."

"I am."

"Anything you want to talk to me about?"

"After the trial."

"Are you going to be there when I talk to J.W.?"

Jerry shook his head. "Nope. He doesn't want me there. Besides which," he said as he looked at his watch, "my team and I are heading off into the wild blue yonder for a weekend of strategic planning without the press for an audience."

"Where are you going?" she asked innocently.

Jerry wagged his finger at her. "You keep trying, don't you?" he said with a smile. "At any rate, J.W. should be back in jail sometime in the next hour. He'll talk to you then."

"Okay. Thanks, Jerry."

By the time Parker had organized his files, the rest of the courtroom had cleared out. He walked back to Shelby and stood looking down at her. "What are you still doing here?"

"I have an appointment with the defendant at the jail in a little while."

"That should help to flesh out your article."

"I certainly hope so."

"Do you mind a little friendly advice?"

His eyes were so incredibly blue. "I won't know until you've offered it."

He didn't smile. "Don't get yourself too involved with this case. Just get the information you need for your article and then back away from it."

"Why?"

"I can't explain it. I just have a bad feeling."

A man she didn't know came to the courtroom door. "Parker, can I see you?"

Parker looked at Shelby for a long moment. Without saying anything else, he walked away from her.

Shelby picked up her purse and went out the other door and down the stairs to the basement of the courthouse where the jail was. It was a stark, brightly lit place. A husky female deputy sat typing behind a semicircular desk.

"Excuse me," Shelby said as she rested her hand on the desk.

The woman looked up.

"My name is Shelby Chassen. I'm here to see Jefferson Webster Lyle."

She nodded and rose. "His attorney told us to expect you. Follow me."

They went down a long corridor that was painted as bright a white as the rest of the courthouse. "Joe!" the woman yelled. "Open up!"

A man stepped up to a barred gate and, with a rattle of his massive key chain, unlocked it and slid it open. The two women walked through. Shelby jumped as it clanked shut behind them.

The woman deputy stopped in front of a steel door that had bars set in a small window. She unlocked it and stepped aside for Shelby to enter. "You have a seat and make yourself comfortable. I'll bring Lyle by in just a minute.''

Shelby sat in a chair facing the door. Reaching into her purse, she took out her recorder, notepad and pen, and waited.

Jail was a noisy place. There was a lot of shouting and clanking.

She kept checking her watch. Nearly half an hour went by before the door opened and Jefferson Webster Lyle entered—in handcuffs. The female deputy smiled at her from over his shoulder. "I'll be right outside if you need me."

The door closed behind her.

J.W. flashed her a flirtatious smile as he straddled the chair across from her. "I'm glad you came, Shelby."

"I'm glad you asked for me."

He inclined his head toward her recorder. "I'd appreciate it if you'd put that away."

Shelby complied. "Do you mind if I take notes?"

"Suit yourself."

"Did you want to see me about something in particular, or is it all right if I ask you questions?"

"A little of both. I want you to know, first of all, that I didn't murder my wife."

"So you said today on the witness stand."

"But you don't believe it?"

"I don't think it matters what I believe."

"It does to me."

"Why?"

"Because you've been sitting in court since jury selection. How do you think it's going?"

"Truthfully I think the prosecution has proved its case."

He shook his head. "Damn. It's not fair. I didn't do it."

"If you didn't, who did?"

"I don't know. I just don't know."

"Why didn't you cooperate with the police when they first began the investigation?"

"Why should I? They started pointing their fingers at me as soon as it happened. There was no presumption of innocence."

"Weren't you interested in finding out who killed Diane?"

J.W. leaned back in his chair. "Look, I'll tell you honestly that our marriage was on shaky ground. Diane was getting ready to leave me, and she was going to take me for every penny she could. Whatever had been between us had died a long time before. I wasn't all that sorry that someone took her out."

Shelby couldn't cover her expression of distaste.

"All right," he said, "I admit I'm not going to win any awards for being Mr. Wonderful. I don't really care what you or anyone else thinks. The point is, whatever I felt about her being killed, I'm not the one who did it."

She looked at him for a long time. "Why did you suddenly agree to see me today? Nothing has altered about my not allowing you to change what I write if you don't like it."

"I know, I know. Jerry told me that you've gotten tight with the prosecutor?"

Shelby blinked in surprise. "I beg your pardon?"

"I want you to talk to him for me."

"Oh, no," she said, shaking her head. "Have your lawyer do it. I'm not here to play go-between for you and the prosecutor."

"Please, Shelby. You have to tell him that I didn't do it. You have to convince him."

Shelby didn't tell him that Parker didn't need convincing. "Look, J.W., your word that you didn't do it isn't enough. Can you think of anything that would point the finger of guilt in a different direction?"

He thought for a long moment. "I really can't. Believe me, I've spent months trying to come up with something—someone."

"Was Diane seeing someone else?"

"Yeah, she was."

Shelby looked at him curiously. "You sound so sure. Did you have someone following her?"

"No, nothing like that. She was getting these phone calls at the house. If I answered, the guy would just hang up or breathe funny into the phone."

"Did you ask Diane about the calls?"

"Sure. She said she didn't have a boyfriend, but I didn't buy it. Jerry and his investigator checked into the boyfriend angle, and found out that she'd just started a relationship with some guy."

"Did they talk to him?"

"Yeah. He had an ironclad alibi. I don't think their relationship had progressed much beyond the talking stage. And he claimed he hadn't made any phone calls to her at our home in Texas. He said she'd asked him not to and that he'd abided by her wishes."

"So we're back to who made the phone calls."

"That's a dead end. You have to remember that this happened more than a year ago."

The jailer opened the door. "Time's up. Let's go, J.W."

"What is it that you want me to do, J.W.?"

He shrugged and got to his feet. "I don't know. I guess I wanted to hear how you thought the trial was going. I already knew, really. And I thought maybe there was something you could do to help influence Kincaid."

"I'm sorry."

"Yeah, well, so's the story of my life." He started from the room, but turned. "I wish we had been able to find the guy making the calls. But how do you find the wind?"

Shelby was suddenly very alert. "What do you mean?"

"That sound he made with his breathing. It was like the wind blowing."

The wind? Like her caller!

She grabbed her things, stuffing them into her shoulder bag as she ran out the door, and made her way gate by gate to the front desk. A man had taken the other jailer's place. She hardly noticed him as she raced past and into the main body of the courthouse, taking the stairs two at a time to Parker's office on the third floor and walking in the door just as he was getting ready to walk out. He grabbed her by the shoulders and smiled into her eyes. "This is a nice surprise, Shelby."

"I need your help."

He was instantly serious. "With what?"

"I was just with J.W. From what he says, Diane was getting calls from the same man who's been calling me."

"How do you know that?"

"Because he described the same eerie sound of the wind that I hear sometimes. It can't just be a coincidence, can it?"

"I don't know." Parker didn't like the sound of this at all. "Let's go back to the jail. I want to talk to J.W. myself."

"Can you do that?" Shelby asked as she tried to keep up with him as they went down the stairs.

"I'll have the jailer call Jerry and ask him to sit in on it."

"You can't do that."

"Why not?"

"Because Jerry has left town. His whole team is gone."

"Then we'll see him without Jerry. As long as J.W.'s willing to talk to me on his own, that should be enough."

The jailer looked up at them as they approached.

"We want to see Jefferson Webster Lyle," Parker said. "Don't bother to bring him to us. Just take us to his cell."

"Yes, sir, Mr. Kincaid." He picked up his phone and pressed three numbers. "Get out here now," he said into the receiver.

Another officer came seemingly out of nowhere a moment later.

"Take Mr. Kincaid here and this lady to J.W. Lyle's cell," the jailer told him. "Stay with them until they're

finished talking to him and bring them back.'' He hit
a button and the gate slid open.

Parker and Shelby followed the officer through a
series of clanging electronic gates and down a long
aisle of narrow but comfortable-looking cells. There
were some appreciative catcalls directed at Shelby. She
reacted by unconsciously moving closer to Parker. His
arm closed protectively around her shoulders as they
walked. When they came to J.W.'s cell, the officer hit
one of the bars. ''J.W., you've got visitors.'' Then he
stepped aside while Shelby and Parker stood outside
the bars looking into the cell.

J.W. looked from one to the other. ''What is it?''

''We want to ask you some questions about the
caller you mentioned to Shelby,'' Parker said.

''Yeah? What about him?'' After all he'd said to
Shelby about wanting the prosecutor's help, his tone
was just short of belligerent.

''How many times did he call that you know of?''
Parker asked, ignoring his tone.

He shrugged. ''Three. Maybe four.''

''Did he ever say anything?''

''Not to me.''

''Did Diane ever talk about the calls?''

''Only to deny that they were from her lover.''

''Were there any other odd things going on with
Diane that you can remember?''

''No. Why are you so interested in this guy?''

''We just are.'' Parker wasn't going to tell him anything. ''If you think of something else, have one of the
officers give me a call. I'll either be at home or in my
office.''

"Wait, there is something," J.W. said as they were turning away. "Diane was misplacing things right and left. Stupid things. And she kept accusing me of taking them. I don't know what the hell she thought I was doing with her perfume and lipstick."

Shelby's fingers dug into Parker's arm.

"Is that it?" Parker asked.

J.W. nodded.

Parker took Shelby by the arm and guided her out of the jail with J.W.'s voice ringing after them as he yelled, "So are you going to help me or what, Kincaid?"

As soon as they were in the waiting area, Parker turned her around to face him. "Have you been missing things?"

"Yes. For months. Perfume. Underwear. Scarves. This afternoon I went to put on some lipstick that I know was in my bathroom this morning, and I couldn't find it anywhere."

"Have you had any phone calls since the last one you told me about?"

"One."

"When was it?"

"The night I had dinner at your house, just before you had the tap put on my phone. He called and told me that I'd betrayed him—just the way *she* had." Shelby's tawny eyes searched his. "Do you think he might have been talking about Diane?"

"It's certainly a possibility."

"Then the man who's calling me might be the one who killed Diane."

Parker turned to the officer behind the desk. "Is Detective Farnsby in?"

"I'll check."

They waited while the officer placed a call. "No, sir," he said after a minute. "He left for home already."

"Put in a call to him and tell him I need to see him back here." He turned to Shelby. "I don't feel good about your staying in that hotel alone."

Shelby smiled at him. "I was just thinking that myself. I'm going to change rooms."

"Or you could come home with me," he suggested. "Danny's anxious to see you play baseball."

Warmth filled her eyes. It was nice that he cared, but she didn't want to be dependent on him. "Danny's a wonderful little boy and it's kind of you to invite me, but I have a lot of writing to do this weekend. I'll be fine on my own. I'd appreciate it if you'd give me a call when and if you find out anything, though."

"Of course I will."

Shelby suddenly felt very shy. "Goodbye. And thanks for helping me."

Parker watched her leave, a worried frown etched on his forehead.

Standing on the steps of the courthouse, Shelby took several deep breaths, unaware of a man standing in the square, watching.

Lost in thought, she crossed the street to the hotel and tried to make arrangements to change her room. There were no vacancies. She went upstairs, and after looking around to see how she could make herself safer, she took two chairs and angled each one under a doorknob to block off both the sitting room and bedroom.

That done, she sat at the table and pulled toward her the pads of notes she'd made during the days of the trial. She spent hours trying to focus completely on her work, going through the notes and making decisions on the direction she wanted the article to take.

Her writing filled page after page.

Time flew by. The room grew dark. She turned on a light and kept writing. The next time she looked at her watch it was eleven o'clock.

She was exhausted. As she tossed her pen onto the table and stretched her arms high over her head, the phone rang. Shelby walked to the phone near the couch and picked up the receiver. "Hello?"

"Hi, Shelby. It's Parker."

"Hi!" she said, happy to hear his drawl as she sank onto the couch.

"I wanted to make sure that you're all right."

"I'm fine. And productive! I got a lot of work done."

"I thought you were going to change rooms."

"They're all full, but I'm quite safe. I barricaded the doors with chairs."

"Shelby, are you sure you won't come home with me?"

"Yes," she said quietly. "Quite sure. As a matter of fact, I was just going to bed."

"All right," he said reluctantly. "But if you change your mind, call me. Otherwise, I'll talk to you tomorrow."

"Good night, Parker," she said softly.

"Good night, princess. Sweet dreams."

She hung up and leaned her head against the back of the couch. Her right hand twisted the gold band on her left around and around.

She was so tired....

Chapter Six

Shelby's eyes flew open at the shrill ringing of the telephone beside the bed. She groped for the receiver in the dark, finally found it and held it to her ear. "Hello?"

"I know who killed her," said a woman's voice.

Shelby, suddenly very much awake, sat up and turned on the light. "Who is this?"

"Who I am isn't important. What matters is that I know who you are."

"Are you saying that J.W. Lyle is innocent?"

"I'm saying that I know who killed Diane Lyle."

"Then you should go to the police."

"Not the police, I want to tell you."

"Then tell me."

"I have to make sure I can trust you first."

"What do you want me to do?"

"Meet me in thirty minutes at the old mill outside of town."

"The old mill? I don't—"

"Thirty minutes. If you're not there on time, I won't wait for you."

"All right. I'll be there. Where is the—"

The line went dead.

Shelby hung up and thought fast. Pulling out the phone directory from the end table, she found Parker's home telephone number and dialed. Rosa answered. "Rosa, I'm sorry to bother you at this hour. It's Shelby Chassen." She pulled clothes out of her drawers while she talked. "I need to talk to Parker."

"Please, don't apologize. I'll get him. Just a minute."

Shelby waited, slipping on jeans and a long-tailed shirt while she switched the receiver from ear to ear.

"I'm sorry, Shelby," Rosa said as she came back on the line, "he's not here. He must still be in his office."

"What's his number there?"

She told her.

"Thanks, Rosa."

Shelby quickly disconnected that call and dialed Parker's office. The phone rang and rang. No answer. Leaving the receiver on her bed with the sound of ringing still coming through, she went to her window and looked at the courthouse. It was completely dark.

She checked her watch; seven minutes had already passed. She didn't have any more time to waste. She had to leave now. Moving fast, she put the receiver back on the hook, grabbed her purse and keys and ran out of the room and down the stairs.

There was no one at the front desk, so she rapidly hit the bell with her hand a few times. A man she'd never seen before came out of a small back room. He'd obviously been eating. "Can I help you?" he asked.

"Yes. I need to know where the old mill is, and I need to know quickly."

"Sure. You take the main street right out of town. Keep going until you get to the, let's see, third road on the left. It's just an old dirt road without any name. I don't think it's very well lit, either. Nothing is out that way."

"So it's on that road?"

He nodded, a reminiscent gleam in his eyes. "About a mile—maybe a mile and a half—down. I haven't been there for years. Not since I was, oh, seven or eight years old and my parents took all of us kids there for a picnic. That was quite a day, I'll tell you. Quite a day. There's a stream nearby. We all took our fishing poles and—"

"I'm really sorry," Shelby interrupted, "but I've got to run." She flew out of the hotel and got into her car. She had the engine running even before her door was closed and shot down the street to the outskirts of town.

She didn't see the man leaning casually against the building, watching her. And she didn't notice that he went into the hotel before she'd gone half a block.

It seemed to take forever before she got to the first road, then forever again before she got to the second one. The third one sort of sneaked up on her and she nearly passed it, but she slammed on the brakes at the last minute and made the turn. Pressing on the accelerator a little harder than she should, she sped down the dirt road, bouncing with every pothole and not noticing. Her headlights finally picked out the old mill, a tumbled-down ruin, a little more than a mile down the road.

Shelby stopped her car and sat perfectly still as she looked around. She couldn't see another car anywhere, though it might have been parked in some nearby trees. Or maybe the woman wasn't here yet. Shelby turned off her headlights and then the engine and waited.

Nothing.

After several minutes she got out of her car and walked around, not venturing far.

It was so quiet.

She held her breath and listened.

A bird suddenly flew out of the trees, noisily flapping its wings and letting out a loud screech. Shelby's heart slammed against her ribs as she whirled toward the sound.

It was quiet again.

"Hello?" she called out tentatively.

There was no answer.

Shelby opened her car door and leaned inside to look at her watch in the overhead light. It had been exactly twenty-eight minutes since she'd gotten the call. She'd wait here fifteen minutes longer and then head back to the hotel if no one showed up.

After closing the door, she paced slowly back and forth alongside her car, waiting for the woman who'd called.

There was no noise. Nothing that would have warned her. Suddenly there was just that whispering voice behind her.

"Hello, Shelby."

She gasped and started to turn, but a strong hand gripped the back of her neck and squeezed, holding her in place.

"I knew you'd come."

Shelby closed her eyes and tried to quell her rising panic. "What do you want from me?"

"You disappointed me, Shelby."

"Disappointed you? What are you talking about?"

"I thought you were different from other women. I loved you more than my own life."

"Who are you?" Despite her best efforts, Shelby's voice was hoarse and frightened-sounding.

The man's hand stroked the back of her neck, sending a shiver of disgust through her body. "I thought we'd have a chance after Eric died, but you betrayed me. Women always betray the men who love them."

Shelby's heart stopped for several beats. "What do you mean, I betrayed you? What are you talking about?"

"I saw you! I saw you through the hotel window, kissing *him,* loving *him.* Then you went home with him. Do you think I don't know what you were doing together?"

Parker, she thought. He had to be talking about Parker.

Shelby suddenly realized that she was crying. She dashed the tears from her cheeks and took a deep breath to calm herself. She had to stay rational. "There's nothing between Mr. Kincaid and myself. We're just acquaintances. If you saw us kissing, there wasn't anything to it other than friendship."

"I saw you." The whisper grew harsh, angry. "Do you take me for a fool?"

She swallowed hard, pushing her fear back. "No," she said, "of course not."

"You've ruined everything, and now you and your lawyer friend are going to pay. Put your hands behind your back."

"No."

He jabbed her in the back with something hard. "I have a gun, Shelby, and believe me when I tell you that I won't hesitate to use it."

She did believe him. There was something in his tone—something in the way he jabbed her with the gun—that told her he wasn't making an idle threat, so she clasped her hands behind her back. A moment later she felt a cord being tightly wound around her wrists.

"What are you going to do to me?"

The man didn't say anything.

"Talk to me, please." She was trying desperately to sound calm.

He wrapped a cloth around her eyes and tied it in a knot at the back of her head.

"Please, I—"

"Enough!" He shoved her hard in the back to get her to move forward.

"Don't do this."

He shoved her again, sending her crashing to her knees. "Where are your keys?"

"In the ignition."

"Stay on the ground."

Shelby heard him open her car door. There was the rattle of keys. Then he grabbed her by her bound wrists and hauled her to her feet. "Come on."

She heard the trunk pop open. He picked her up bodily and dumped her inside, then slammed the lid down. There was another rattle of keys that sounded as though they'd been dropped. She could hear sirens wailing faintly in the distance.

The man swore. She heard someone running. The footsteps were loud at first, then gradually faded until she couldn't hear them any longer.

Then there were other noises. A car barreling down the road and sliding on the dirt and gravel to a stop. A car door opened and slammed shut. "Shelby!" yelled a voice she was growing more and more fond of.

"Parker," she screamed, relieved beyond belief. "I'm in the trunk."

"Are you all right?" he yelled.

"Yes, just get me out of here."

"Where are the keys?"

"I don't know. It sounded like he dropped them. Are you sure he's gone?"

"There's no one here. I've got them."

A moment later he opened the trunk and lifted her out just as several police cars came roaring down the road, lights flashing. Parker took off her blindfold, then turned her around and unbound her wrists.

As soon as she was free, he wrapped her in his arms. "Are you sure you're all right?"

"I am now." She'd never felt more safe than she did at that moment, in his arms. "How did you know where I was?"

"When I got home, Rosa told me you'd called. I tried calling you back, and when I couldn't get a hold of you, I asked the clerk if he knew where you were. He told me you'd asked about the old mill. I called the police and came straight here."

"Thank God you did. I think he was going to kill me."

He held her away from him and looked down at her. "Why? Who was he? And why on earth would you come out here alone?"

"A woman called me and said she knew who'd killed Diane. It never occurred to me that there was any danger. I thought she just wanted to talk. When I got here, there was no woman. It was the man who's been calling me."

Parker pulled her back into his arms and held her close.

"He was going to kill me!"

"We're going to find him, Shelby. This man has tormented you long enough. I'm not going to allow him to do this to you any longer."

She leaned back in his arms and looked up at him, her eyes full of fear. The policemen had scattered in all directions following paths lit from them by both their headlights and flashlights. "I think he's going to come after you, too, Parker. He thinks we're having an affair. He said that I betrayed him with you.''

A corner of his mouth lifted. ''I wish.''

''Parker, he means it. The man is crazy.''

''You let me worry about that.'' He pushed her hair away from her face. ''I'm not going to let anything happen to you or me.''

''I'm frightened.''

He pressed his lips against her forehead. ''I know,'' he said softly. ''But you won't have to be frightened for long. We're going to find him and put him where he belongs so he can't hurt anyone ever again.''

Shelby sighed.

''Come on. You're going to stay with me for the rest of the time you're in Dry River Falls. We'll pick up your things tomorrow.''

She wasn't about to argue.

Parker helped her into the pickup truck. ''Oh,'' she said suddenly, ''what about my car?''

''The police will bring it over later.'' He closed the door and looked at her through the open window. ''Wait here for a minute. I want to talk to one of the officers.''

Shelby's eyes followed him through the moonlight to her car where an officer was going over the trunk with his flashlight. They talked for a while, but Shelby's gaze never wavered. It was as though she felt that as long as she could see Parker, everything would be all right.

Then Parker came back to the truck and climbed into the driver's side. He didn't say anything as he turned the truck around and headed for his ranch.

Shelby didn't say anything either. She was beyond words.

When they got to the ranch, Parker opened the door for Shelby and lifted her out of the truck, gently setting her on the ground. Still without speaking, they went into the house. Rosa came rushing into the living room. "Will you tell me what's going on?" she asked Parker. "The way you rushed out of here!"

"It's a long story, Rosa. Suffice to say that I went to get Shelby. She's going to be staying with us for a while."

Rosa looked at Shelby. "Are you all right, dear?"

"I'm fine now."

She wagged her finger at Parker. "There's a lot more to this than your simply going to get Shelby. I want to know what's happening."

"I'll tell you tomorrow. Right now I think we could all use some rest. Is the guest room ready?"

Rosa's mouth was set in a resigned line. "Not yet, but it will be."

"Rosa," Shelby said, "I'm sorry that I keep intruding on you like this. You've been very patient."

The resigned line turned up at the corners. "Please don't give it a thought. You're always welcome here, whatever the circumstances. I'd just like to know what's going on." She reached out and hugged Shelby. "I'll get your room ready."

"Thanks."

The housekeeper started up the stairs.

"Rosa," Parker said. "Would you please check on Danny before you go back to bed?"

"All right."

He looked down at Shelby. "I don't know about you, but I could use a drink."

"I think I'd like one, too."

She followed him into the kitchen and sat on a stool while he reached into a high cabinet and took out some bottles.

"I have Scotch, brandy, bourbon, cognac and—" he looked at the last bottle "—tequila."

"Brandy, please."

He poured her a brandy and a Scotch for himself, then sat across the counter from her. "I want you to give me a chronology of your contacts with this man who grabbed you tonight. When did the calls start?"

She sipped the brandy and let it burn its way down her throat. "The day of Eric's funeral."

"What did he say?"

"Just my name."

"Anything else?"

She shook her head. "No."

"All right. When was the next call?"

Shelby stared into her brandy glass. "A few weeks after that. Again, he said my name over and over again, and then the calls started coming every week— sometimes every day. Occasionally he just said my name, and other times there was just the sound of the wind. Finally I went to the police. They tried to trace his calls, but the most they ever found out was that the guy was calling from pay phones."

"I noticed from the records I got that they pretty much gave up on catching him."

"We all did. I think we all kind of relaxed, because though the calls kept coming, there was never any threat. But now there *is* a threat, and you've been pulled right into the middle of it." She shook her head. "It's all my fault."

Parker walked around the counter and lifted her from the stool into his arms. "Shelby, you aren't responsible for a crazy man's actions."

"I don't want anything to happen to you because of me," she said softly.

"You let me worry about that."

"But, Parker...."

"Shh." He lowered his mouth to hers and kissed her deeply. His hands slid to the curve of her slender waist and pulled her body close to his before wrapping her in his strong arms.

Shelby was beyond any kind of resistance. It was wonderful to be in his arms, and she let herself feel wonderful about it. It was only then that she realized how many times she'd thought about what it would be like to be close to him like this.

Parker raised his head and looked tenderly into her eyes. "Do you have any idea how much I want you? How much I've wanted you since the first moment I saw you?"

She raised her head and traced his lips with her fingertip. Everything—everyone—was forgotten but this man. She was hungry for him, for his touch, in a way she'd never experienced before. There was no shyness. No hesitation. Just a raw need building inside her. Looking at him made her blood surge through her veins.

Shelby's eyes were like mirrors to the man holding her. Every thought and emotion was relayed to him.

Still looking into those eyes, he raised his hand and began to unbutton her blouse with slow deliberation. His hand brushed against her already-sensitive breast. Shelby inhaled softly and closed her eyes as she tilted her head back, exposing the long line of her throat. Parker kissed her lingeringly, working his way from her earlobe to the soft swell of her breast, tasting her, inhaling the soft perfume of her skin.

Shelby tangled her fingers in his thick hair, loving the feel of it, pressing his mouth more tightly to her.

Parker straightened suddenly, covering her lips with his as he lifted her onto the edge of the high stool and moved between her legs. His tongue slowly probed every corner of her mouth. Shelby wrapped her legs around him, pulling him against her—against the ache that had taken over her body so completely that she was helpless against its power. She could feel him pressing against her, his need every bit as great as hers. She wanted him closer. Parker groaned against her mouth.

Neither of them heard the knock at the front door until whoever was out there hammered on it with his fist.

Parker raised his head and looked into her eyes. Both of them were breathing hard.

"Parker!" a man yelled, "it's me, Craig." He knocked again. "Open the door."

Shelby raised a hand to her throat. Her pulse was throbbing. "Who's Craig?" she asked, trying to focus her thoughts.

"A policeman." Parker still in the circle of her legs, pulled her back into his arms and held her, trying to regain some control over his body before moving.

"Don't go," she whispered against his ear. "Don't leave me."

Parker leaned away from her. Taking her face in his hands, he kissed her tenderly. "I have to talk to him. He may have caught the man who attacked you tonight."

Shelby lowered her legs and looked down.

"Don't do that, honey," Parker said as he raised her head so her eyes met his. "Don't retreat from me now. Don't let that wall you've built around yourself come between us again."

She didn't say anything, and he couldn't follow it up because at that moment there was another knock at the door.

"I'll be right back."

Shelby raised a shaking hand to straighten her blouse. She saw a glint of gold and held out her left hand.

The wedding band.

How could she do this to Eric? It wasn't fair that he was dead and she was moving on with her life. How could she just set him aside as though he'd never existed and fall in love with a man she'd known for only a few days?

But that wasn't the worst betrayal. Tonight, for the first time in her life, Shelby had learned what it was to want a man. To want him so badly that it overwhelmed everything else. She'd never dreamed that she could feel that way. She *had* loved Eric. But making love had never been an important part of their relationship. Theirs had been more a meeting of minds; a comfortableness in each other's company. If Eric had still been alive, there was no doubt in Shelby's mind that what she had with him would have been enough for her. She never would have known any other way.

But now there was Parker.

Her eyes filled with hot tears. "Oh, Eric," she whispered, "I'm so sorry."

The low vibration of men's voices in the living room cut through her cloud of sadness. She walked over to the sink and ran cool water over her fingers, then raised them to her eyes and held them there.

Taking a deep breath, she straightened her shoulders and walked into the living room. A policeman stood just inside the door talking to Parker.

Shelby cleared her throat. "What's going on?" she asked without looking at Parker. "Did you find him?"

The officer shook his head. "I'm afraid not, ma'am, but we found where we think he parked his car, about a mile down the road from where you were. I know that doesn't help much, and I wish I had better news for you. I'm sorry."

"Please don't be sorry," she said. "No one has been able to catch this man for nearly a year."

"Maybe we'll get lucky, ma'am."

"I hope so."

"When you were with him," the officer asked, "did he say anything about Diane Lyle?"

She shook her head. "Not a word."

"Okay. Well," he said to Parker, "I'm going back out. We've got a couple of men watching your property. Ya'll keep a good thought. I'll call you if anything breaks."

"Good night, Craig," Parker said as he shook the officer's hand. "Thanks." As soon as he'd gone, Parker closed the door and turned to Shelby. "We will catch him."

She nodded. "I know."

He tenderly touched her cheek. "You look tired," he said quietly.

"I am."

He took her by the hand. "Come on. I'll show you to your room."

They went upstairs together. "This is Danny's room," he said, pointing to the first door they passed. "The next one is Rosa's. This one is yours." He stopped in front of the door and opened it.

"Thank you."

"There are two bathrooms in the hall. Use whichever one you want. Knowing Rosa, she's probably already put towels and a toothbrush in your bedroom." He looked at her more closely in the dim light of the hallway. "Are you all right?"

She avoided his eyes. "I will be."

He leaned over and gently kissed the top of her head. "If you need anything during the night, just call out and I'll hear you. I'm right next door."

She nodded.

"Good night."

"Night." She went into the room and closed the door. For a long time she stood in the dark, leaning against the door. Just as she started to move, she heard Parker say her name. She opened the door and found him standing there holding one of his shirts.

"I thought you might need something to sleep in," he said, holding it out to her.

"Thank you."

"Good night again."

This time when she closed the door, she flipped on the wall switch. A small bedside lamp illuminated a really charming room. The bed, with its patchwork quilt on top, was invitingly turned back. There was a small desk, a dresser and a rocking chair set near the window. Shelby undressed and draped her clothes over the rocker. Then she slipped on Parker's shirt and rolled up the sleeves. It felt good against her skin.

Instead of going straight to bed, she turned out the lamp and walked to the window. Leaning her shoulder against the frame, she crossed her arms over her breasts and stared outside. It was pitch-black out, just before dawn. She didn't see the officers, but then she hadn't really expected to.

She stayed there for a long time, deep in thought.

Just as the sky began to brighten with an orange sunrise, she crossed to the bed and sank onto the mattress.

She was so tired.

Her eyes drifted closed.

Parker didn't even bother to turn on the light in his room. He just laid on the bed in his clothes, his hands beneath his head, and stared up at the dark ceiling, going over in his mind everything that had happened that day.

He heard the bedsprings creak in Shelby's room when she finally lay down.

He turned his head and stared at the wall beyond which she lay. "I won't let that man hurt you, Shelby," he said quietly. "I won't let anyone ever hurt you again."

Chapter Seven

Shelby shot up in bed, her heart pounding. Was it a dream or had she heard something?

She heard it again. A car door slamming. She climbed out of bed and walked to the window. Holding the curtain aside with her hand, she could see Parker standing in the driveway talking to two policemen. Danny was outside, too, racing around with his puppy. Maybe they'd caught the man.

She quickly put on her jeans and ran barefoot downstairs and out the front door to Parker's side.

He looked down at her and smiled. It was impossible not to. Her hair was mussed, her cheeks flushed, and she could have gone swimming in his shirt.

"What's going on?" she asked.

"Nothing, I'm afraid," one of the policemen said. "We've run out of places to look. We're not giving up, of course, but at this time there's nothing new to tell you."

Her shoulders sagged a little. "I see."

"After we went over your car, we took it back to the hotel. The clerk has the keys."

"Thank you."

"I'm sorry we don't have better news for you."

Shelby managed a smile. "I know you're doing all you can. Thank you."

The one who'd been doing the talking looked at Parker. "We'll let you know if we turn up anything. In the meantime, we're going to keep two officers here, and we'll have one that will go everywhere Miss Chassen goes."

They watched as the two officers climbed into their squad car, turned it around and drove away.

Parker put his arm around her shoulders and turned her toward the house. "I was hoping you'd be able to sleep a little longer."

"I heard the car."

"It's still early. You can go back to bed if you want."

She shook her head. "No, that's all right. I want to talk to you anyway."

"About?"

"I'm not going to stay here."

He stopped walking and turned her toward him. "Of course you are."

"No, I'm not. I don't know what I was thinking last night." She looked into his eyes, and there was no mistaking her meaning. "I suppose I wasn't thinking at all. I just can't stay here."

Parker was torn. He wanted to protect her, but at the same time he didn't want her to feel like his prisoner. "So what do you propose to do?"

"I don't know yet. Maybe I'll just pack up my things and go back to Vermont."

"Honey, you can't handle this alone."

"I have so far."

"But you don't have to anymore. I'm here and I want to help you."

Shelby couldn't help herself. She reached out and touched his beard-shadowed cheek. "I've dragged you into this mess. Now you and Danny and Rosa are all at risk. It's not right."

"You didn't drag anybody into anything. If this man is the one who killed Diane Lyle, then regardless of anything else, he has to be caught and I'm the one who's going to prosecute him. That has nothing to do with you."

"I still want you to take me back to the hotel today."

Danny ran over to them, his bat and ball in hand. "Hi, Shelby! Do you want to play ball with my dad and me?"

Shelby and Parker continued staring at each other.

"Hey," Danny said as he pulled on Shelby's hand, "do you want to play baseball? We can take turns batting."

She tore her gaze away from Parker's and smiled down at the little boy. "Sure, Danny. I'll go put my shoes on and be right back."

"Okay, Dad?"

Parker was annoyed with Shelby, but he pushed his feelings aside when he looked at his son. "All right." He ruffled Danny's hair. "Do you want to pitch or bat first?"

When Shelby came out a few minutes later, Danny ran up to her with the bat, the puppy at his heels. "It's your turn."

She took the bat and shook her head. "I hope your expectations aren't too high. I only did this for one summer, and it was a long time ago."

"Just do the best you can," Danny told her seriously as he patted her arm. "No one can ask more of you than that."

The child absolutely melted her heart. "Where should I stand?" she asked.

He pointed to a spot about twenty feet away where a Frisbee had been dropped to indicate home plate. "I'll pitch and Dad will be outfield." He looked out to where Parker was standing. "Dad!" he yelled, "you might want to bring up the outfield a little bit."

Parker moved in closer as Shelby took her place and got ready to bat.

"That's a pretty good stance," Danny said approvingly. "Ready?"

"Ready."

"I won't throw too hard."

"Thank you."

He wound up and let it fly. Shelby swung and missed, then had to chase the ball because there wasn't a catcher.

"That's okay," Danny said encouragingly when she tossed the ball back to him. "Try again."

This time she gave the ball a good solid smack that sent it high into the air and over Parker's head. He had to run for it, but he caught it and threw it back to Danny.

"You would have been out," Danny told her, "but it was a really good hit. You bat a few more times and then we'll switch positions."

Fifteen minutes later, Shelby had been rotated to the outfield, all the while avoiding Parker's eyes, when Rosa stepped onto the porch. "Breakfast, everyone!"

"Can we play a little longer?" Danny asked.

"No. It'll get cold. Come on in."

He wrinkled his nose. "All right." He went ahead of them, the puppy following.

Parker waited for Shelby. "We need to talk."

She shook her head, avoiding his eyes. "I'm through talking. And if it's all right with you, I'd just as soon skip breakfast and go straight back to the hotel."

Parker leveled his eyes at her. "Why are you doing this?"

"I need time to myself."

"You mean that you need to put some distance between the two of us."

She didn't answer.

"You're putting up a barrier between us that shouldn't be there. Especially not after last night."

Her throat tightened. "Last night was a mistake."

"For whom?"

"Both of us."

"Oh, no, Shelby. You know better."

Shelby passed him to walk into the house. "I don't want to talk about this."

He caught her arm and swung her around. "What is it with you? You're in a constant state of denial. Do you think if you tell yourself often enough that you don't feel something, you won't feel it? Do you think if you deny what happened between us last night that it will go away?"

"I don't know what I think anymore—I don't know what I feel. I only know that I have to get away from here."

"Now I understand," Parker said quietly.

"You understand what?"

"You're not running from the man who attacked you last night, you're running away from me."

"Stop turning everything around."

"Am I doing that, or are you?"

Shelby was so confused that she didn't know why she was doing anything anymore. She couldn't analyze it. She didn't want to talk about it. "May we go now?" she asked without missing a beat.

Parker sighed and let go of her arm. "I'll tell Rosa. You get in the truck."

"Thank you."

She walked to the truck and climbed inside. A policeman she hadn't noticed until that moment came over to her and leaned his arms on the open window. "Where are you going, ma'am?"

"Mr. Kincaid is taking me back to my hotel."

"Do you want me to follow you?"

"No. I'd rather that you stay here with Danny and Rosa."

He inclined his head and wandered off, whistling as he walked.

Shelby leaned back in her seat. Her eyes followed Parker as he came out of the house and walked toward the truck. His faded jeans fit perfectly over his muscled thighs.

He got in without saying anything and started the engine. Turning his head, he looked at her for a long moment, then put the truck into gear and headed toward town.

Shelby stared out the passenger window, her thoughts and emotions in such turmoil that she didn't really see anything.

When they got to the hotel, she climbed out on her own and headed inside, but Parker caught up with her and, still in silence, walked her up the stairs to her door. She took the key out of her pocket and inserted it in the lock, turning the knob and opening the door a crack. "Goodbye," she said, looking up at Parker.

The muscle in his jaw tightened. "For now."

She opened the door farther and went into her room. Parker was already halfway down the hall when he heard her scream. He ran back and found Shelby standing in the middle of a scene of complete devastation. Papers were strewn everywhere. Her clothes had been shredded and thrown from one end of the suite to the other. Furniture was overturned and lamps were broken. "Bang, bang, Shelby," was written on the wall in lipstick.

"That son of a..." Parker caught himself and looked at Shelby. She was walking around the room like a lost little girl, picking up the ruins of her things and holding them in her arms. He went straight to the phone and called the police. Then he called Rosa.

When he'd finished, he went to Shelby and, with his hands on her shoulders, pressed her down onto the only cushion that was still on the couch. "All right, you told me what you want to do. Now I'm going to tell you the way it's going to be. I've just told Rosa to pack up herself and Danny and go visit her sister in Arizona until she hears from me. You are going to move into the house with me, and we're going to wait there together for this nut to come after us. It's the only way we're going to catch him, Shelby. Surely you can see that."

She swallowed hard and looked around the room.

"He's not going to just quit, honey." The endearment slipped from Parker as naturally as his breath. "Things have gone too far. We have to stop him."

There was a knock on the open door. "Shelby, I—"

She and Parker looked up to find Charles standing in the doorway. He looked around in disbelief. "What the hell happened in here? Did you have a party and forget to invite me?" he asked as he stepped over a broken lamp.

"Don't joke around, Charles. I'm not in the mood." Shelby picked up a skirt from the couch. It had been slashed from waist to hem.

The photographer was suddenly serious. "What *did* happen here?"

Shelby just shook her head. "I can't believe this. It has to be that guy who has been calling me."

Parker headed out of the room. "Pack whatever you can salvage. I'll be back in a few minutes. Charles, you stay with her until the police arrive."

"Sure."

Shelby rose from the couch and walked around as though in a daze, picking up her things and stacking them in the middle of the floor. Not all of her clothes had been torn. She put those in a separate pile.

Charles helped her, picking up her notebooks and loose papers and putting them on the table. "What are you going to do now?" he asked. "The trial still has at least a week to go."

"I guess I'm going to move in with Parker."

"Move in with him?"

She didn't explain. "Would you get my suitcase out of the bedroom for me, Charles?"

"Sure." He disappeared into the bedroom and came back out a minute later.

"Did he do anything to it?"

Charles examined the suitcase inside and out. "No."

With a sigh, she picked up an armful of clothes and dumped them into it.

Charles watched her with concern. "Do you want me to stay in Dry River Falls with you, Shelby?"

She managed to smile at him, and touched his arm. "That's very sweet of you, but no."

"Really, I can stay if you want me to."

"No, no. You go. I'll be fine."

"Are you sure?"

She nodded. "I think I've got almost too many people looking out for me."

Several policemen walked in and looked around. One of them whistled in amazement, then started telling the others what to do. Charles leaned over and shyly kissed Shelby on the cheek. "I'm going to head out now. If you need me for anything, call the office. They'll know where to reach me."

"Thanks, Charles. I appreciate that."

Parker came back in just as Charles was leaving. "Have you got everything?" he asked her.

"Let me just check in the bedroom and bathroom."

"Okay."

While she collected what was left of her makeup and clothing, Parker talked to the policemen.

She came out of the bedroom a few minutes later and dropped the rest of her things into the suitcase. "That's it."

Parker snapped it shut and picked it up. "Let's go."

She wasn't going to argue anymore.

"I talked to that detective I called last night from the jail. He's been looking into the connections between you and Diane from work."

"There must be dozens of them."

"That's right."

"But he hasn't spoken with me. How does he know who I've had dealings with?"

"He has the Vermont police file that I sent for along with your personnel file from your publisher. He and another detective are comparing the names in your file with the names in Diane's file. Some are obviously not your caller. Others aren't so obvious."

"Don't forget that the person who called me last night was a woman."

"We already know who she is."

They walked through the lobby and out to the truck. Parker put her suitcase in back, helped her in, climbed into the driver's seat and pulled away from the curb.

"Well?" she asked impatiently.

"It was Lyle's sister."

"Lyle's sister? Why would she set me up with that man?"

"She wasn't even thinking about what was going to happen to you. She got a call from a man telling her that he'd help get her brother off if she'd do a favor for him."

"And that favor was to call me."

"Exactly."

"And no doubt she doesn't know who the man was."

"Doesn't have a clue. She heard through the grapevine about what happened to you last night and showed up at the police station to tell them what she knew. She says that she didn't mean you any harm."

Shelby sighed. Lots was happening, but nothing was getting any clearer.

When they got to the ranch, Rosa was putting the puppy carrier into the back of a police car. Danny came racing out of the house and threw himself into Parker's arms, where he hung happily and looked at Shelby. "Hi, guys! Did Rosa tell you what we're doing?" he asked excitedly. "We're riding in a real police car to the airport!"

Parker hugged him. "I know." He looked over the top of his son's head to his housekeeper. "Your tickets are waiting for you at the counter."

She nodded. "Come on, Danny. We have to leave."

Parker set him on the ground, and Danny ran around the truck to hug Shelby. "Will you be here when we get back?"

She smiled down at him and pushed his hair off his forehead. "I don't think so, Danny."

His smile faded. "Why not?"

"I have to go back to my own home."

"You could live here. We have lots of room."

"Thank you, Danny. That's a very generous offer."

"So you'll think about it?"

"Well . . ."

He crooked his finger at her to get her to lean toward him. "I think my dad likes you," he whispered in her ear.

"Danny," Rosa said in exasperation, "come on. We have to go."

He grinned at Shelby as though they had a secret understanding and ran to the police car.

Rosa kissed Parker on the cheek, then went to Shelby and took one of Shelby's hands in both of hers. "Everything's going to be fine. And who knows," she said, looking meaningfully from one to the other, "maybe something good will come out of all this. You two be careful."

"We will." Parker helped her into the police car and closed the door after her.

Danny turned in his seat and waved to them through the rear window as the car headed down the driveway.

As soon as it was out of sight, Parker leaned into the truck and took a gun out of the glove compartment. "Have you ever fired one of these?" he asked as he showed it to Shelby.

She looked at it in distaste. "No."

"Somehow that doesn't surprise me. You're about to get a crash course in how to handle a gun."

"Where did you get it?"

"It's mine. I keep it at the office instead of the house because of Danny. Come on."

Shelby followed him several hundred yards down a small hill to a barn she hadn't even known was there. Parker disappeared into the barn and came out a minute later with a large sheet of plywood that he leaned against a fence. "All right. Let's get to work. This is how you hold it."

She studied his hands, and when he handed the gun to her, did exactly what he had done, with her right index finger on the trigger and her left hand cupping the butt of the gun. "How's this?" she asked.

"Very good. Now, when you go to fire the gun, hold your arms out straight from your body and high enough so that you can sight down the barrel."

She raised her arms and closed one eye as she looked down the barrel. "It's heavy."

Parker stood behind her, his arms around her, his hands on hers as he adjusted her grip slightly and helped her hold it up. "Too heavy?"

Shelby was trying not to think about her back pressed against his chest. "No, although I don't think I'd be able to hold it this high for very long."

"Hopefully you won't have to do this at all after today. I just want you to have the means to protect yourself if you need to." He moved away from her. "Have you got the plywood sighted?"

She nodded.

"All right. Slowly squeeze the trigger with your index finger. The gun is going to jump, but don't let that worry you. You'll get used to it."

Shelby pulled back slowly on the trigger, just as he said. Nothing could have prepared her for the loud boom that cracked through the air and echoed off the trees. She opened her eyes and looked for a hole in the board. "Did I hit it?"

Parker flashed her a wry look. "Of course you didn't. You had your eyes closed."

"I did not!"

He pinched her chin and smiled his lazy smile. "Yes, my dear, you did. I know that because *my* eyes happened to be open. Try again."

"Couldn't I just throw the gun at him?"

Parker's smile grew. "Come on."

With a sigh, Shelby raised the gun and took another shot. And another. And another.

He kept her at it for more than an hour until she could hit the middle of the board more times than she missed it. After the last shot, he took the gun from her. "Now that you know how to shoot a gun, do you think you'll be able to use it if it becomes necessary to defend yourself?"

She thought about his question. "If you'd asked me that a year go, I probably would have answered no. But now, I honestly think I could."

"Good, because you may have to. I want you to keep it near you until the guy is caught."

"All right." She was quiet for a moment. "Do you really think he'll come?"

"I don't know."

"I hope he does. I'd like to get this nightmare over with so I can get on with my life."

Their gazes met and locked.

Chapter Eight

As Parker lay in bed that night, he could hear Shelby pacing in the next room. She'd been at it ever since they'd gone to bed more than an hour earlier. Every once in a while she'd stop, just for a few moments, and then the pacing would start again.

Finally, bare-chested, wearing only drawstring pajama bottoms, he got up and went to her room.

"Yes?" Shelby said when she heard him knock.

He pushed the door open and stood looking at her in the dim light of her bedside lamp. Her nightgown had been slashed, so she was wearing another one of Parker's shirts. It came to about the middle of her thigh, leaving the rest of her long legs bare.

His eyes moved slowly down her body, then back to her eyes. "Are you going to be moving around all night?" he asked.

Shelby looked at him, chagrined. "I'm sorry. I didn't know you could hear me."

"Well, I can. What's wrong?"

"I can't sleep."

"So I gathered."

"I'll stop pacing."

"I know you will. You're coming with me."

"Excuse me?"

He walked into the room and took her by the hand. "Come on, Shelby."

"Will you stop that!" she said, digging her bare heels into the carpeting. "You're always pulling me places."

"That's because you never seem to go anywhere willingly. Either come with me now or I'll carry you. The choice is yours."

Shelby, with a look Parker found difficult to interpret—which was perhaps just as well—let him lead her to his bedroom.

"Lie down," he said.

She shook her head. "I don't think so."

"Oh, for heaven's sake, I'm not going to ravish you. This is the only way either of us is going to get any sleep."

"I..."

Parker picked her up bodily and deposited her onto his bed. "There. That wasn't so difficult, was it?"

She eyed him warily.

Parker lay on the bed beside her, slipping his arm around her and settling her cheek against his shoulder. "All right so far?" he asked quietly, his lips against the top of her head.

"Is this it?"

"For tonight, yes." She could hear the smile in his voice. "You can feel free to relax."

Shelby lay in his arms like a statue, but as time passed and he didn't move, she did relax. Protected by the darkness, she felt freer.

"Parker?"

"Umm?"

"Why haven't you ever married?"

"I suppose because you were living somewhere else and I couldn't find you."

"I'm serious."

"So am I, Shelby." There was no smile in his voice.

She put her hand on his chest. They lay in silence for a long time. "Talk to me," Shelby said into the darkness.

"About what?"

"Yourself. I don't know anything about you except how Danny came to be your son. Where were you born?"

"Houston."

"Are your parents still living?"

"No. My mother died when I was six. My father died when I was in college."

"I'm sorry."

He didn't say anything.

"What was your childhood like?"

"Except for when my mom died, I had a terrific childhood."

"Did you always want to be an attorney?"

She could feel him smile. "I was just like Danny. Baseball was my life. I was already in college when I decided on law."

"Jerry told me that you used to be a really good criminal defense lawyer in Houston."

"He's right."

"What made you decide to become a prosecutor?"

"It's a long story, Shelby."

"We have all night."

Parker rubbed his cheek against her hair. "The condensed version is that I got a client acquitted who was accused of rape. Within two weeks of getting back on the street, he did it again and wanted me to represent him. It turned my stomach."

"Things like that must happen to most criminal defense attorneys."

"I'm sure it does. But I couldn't handle it and didn't want to have to handle it in the future. I became a prosecutor because it gave me the best of both worlds. If someone's guilty, I can put him away. If he's not, I don't prosecute."

"Except for J. W. Lyle."

"Yeah. Good old J.W. There's always an exception somewhere down the line."

"What's going to happen if the man who attacked me and the man who killed Diane Lyle don't turn out to be the same?"

"My hands will be tied. I have lots of evidence that says J.W. killed his wife and none that says he didn't. My instincts could be wrong, and J.W. could be as guilty as guilty can be. That's not for me to decide. It's up to that jury. And I guess the rest of us can keep looking." He kissed the top of her head and sighed. "Try to get some sleep."

Shelby closed her eyes. For the first time in more than a year, she felt completely safe. No one could hurt her while she was lying in Parker's arms.

Parker listened to her breathing as it grew soft and even. *Shelby,* he thought. *Do you have any idea how you've turned my world upside down?*

Shelby slept through the night and well into the morning. Even after she awakened, she lay in the quiet room with her eyes closed, savoring the feeling of being well-rested.

Parker.

She opened her eyes and turned her head to look beside her. He wasn't there. Rolling onto her stomach, she buried her face in his pillow, surrounding herself with the clean, masculine smell of him.

Nothing in her life had prepared Shelby for the way she felt about Parker Kincaid.

Or the almost overwhelming guilt attached to those feelings.

Shelby climbed out of bed and went back to her own room to get some cuffed shorts and a T-shirt that had escaped the whisperer's attention. Rosa had left towels on the dresser, and she took them with her into the bathroom to use after her shower. When she was clean and dressed, she went downstairs. There was a policeman sitting in the living room. He rose and smiled at her. "Afternoon, ma'am."

"Hi," she said with a smile. "Where's Parker?"

"He wanted me to tell you that he's working on a fence in one of the pastures. I can take you to him if you want."

"You don't have to do that. Just tell me where he is and I'll find him."

"I'm afraid I can't do that, ma'am. I have orders to stay with you at all times unless you're with Mr. Kincaid."

"I see. Well, then thank you. I'd appreciate your taking me to him."

They went outside together and climbed into the squad car he'd parked next to the house.

It was a beautiful day. Hot, yes, but not uncomfortably so. The sky was clear, a beautiful deep blue. The air was fresh. And she could see forever.

They drove past the barn and along a lengthy stretch of pasture that was fenced in. She saw some horses and a few cattle.

"There he is," the officer said, pointing.

Parker, shirtless, had his back to them as he raised a sledgehammer high over his head and brought it down on a fencepost. His chiseled arms and shoulders glistened with sweat.

The officer stopped the car a few feet from the fence. Parker turned and smiled at her as she climbed out. "Do you want me to stay here?" the officer yelled out the window.

Parker's eyes, as blue as the Texas sky, never left Shelby. "No. We'll be all right. Go back to the house."

The officer turned his car around and drove slowly back down the narrow dirt track.

Shelby walked to Parker, stopping in front of him on the other side of the fence. "You're staring," she said with just a hint of embarrassed color in her cheeks.

His gaze caressed her, warming her from the inside out. "Every time I see you, you take my breath away."

Shelby lowered her eyes, not knowing what to say.

"I watched you sleeping this morning."

"You should have awakened me."

"I thought I already had—a little."

Her eyes flew to his.

Parker's mouth curved in a slow smile, deepening the creases in his cheeks. "For a woman who projects such a sophisticated, worldly image, you blush with remarkable ease."

"What one sees isn't always what one gets."

"So I've learned."

Shelby looked down the long line of fence. There were more than a dozen new posts in place.

He followed her gaze. "Now you know what exciting things I do with my weekends," he said, "when I'm not taking care of damsels in distress."

"This is a wonderful place. I hope I have a chance to see more of it before I go back to Vermont."

Parker let that remark slide by. "It's not very large, as ranches around here go. Even so, it's a lot to take care of."

"Do you have help?"

"One full-time and two part-time workers."

Shelby closed her eyes and raised her face to the sun, enjoying the brightness and heat.

"Don't do that very long with that skin of yours. As a matter of fact," he said, "why don't you go sit under that tree over there until I finish what I'm doing."

"I'd rather wander around, if that's all right."

"I want to keep an eye on you."

"It's strange. I don't know if it's the sunlight, you or the wide open spaces, but out here I'm not afraid at all."

"I'm glad you're not afraid, but don't let that make you incautious."

"Would it be all right if I just went into the next pasture? I saw some horses there."

"All right. Don't go too far."

Shelby smiled at him. "I'm not a child."

"Believe me, I'm very well aware of that."

His eyes followed her as she climbed over a finished portion of fence bordering the next pasture and headed across it toward the spot where she'd last seen the horses. He liked watching her walk. For all that she moved with the grace of a lady, there was a little bit of a suppressed tomboy in her that he found extremely appealing.

True to her word, she stayed in his line of vision, stopping several hundred yards away and clapping her hands. The horses, curious creatures that they were, made their way slowly to her, grazing as they came, stopping occasionally to assess the situation.

Shelby sat in the dry grass and waited for them to come to her, and they eventually did, Parker noted with amusement—mother, father and colt. The father stopped some distance away, his nostrils flaring as he sniffed the air. The mother ventured closer, mostly because she had to if she wanted to keep up with her son. The colt ran right up to her, ready to play.

Shelby laughed as she stroked his silky nose. "Oh, you're a beautiful little thing. How old are you?"

Parker had finished the post he'd been working on and walked up behind her. "Six weeks."

She looked over her shoulder, her eyes alight.

"I'm his official spokesman," he explained.

Shelby laughed out loud. "What's his name?" she asked as she turned to him, her arm around the back of the colt's neck.

"DiMaggio."

"DiMaggio?" She looked at the colt with a small frown. "That's an odd name for a horse."

"Maybe, but it's a great name for a baseball player."

"Oh, no," she said with a grin. "You let Danny name him."

"I did, indeed. And as you may have gathered, he's been studying baseball history."

A cloud suddenly moved across the sky, blocking the sun for a minute.

"Where did that come from?" Shelby asked as she looked up.

Parker looked up, too, and saw that lots of clouds had started gathering and they were getting darker. "We'd better get back to the house. Storms around here have a habit of coming on rather suddenly."

"What about the horses?" she asked, her arm still around the colt.

"They have a shelter at the other end of the pasture. They know when they need to use it. Come on." He took her hand. "And this time I promise not to pull you if you come along on your own."

Shelby smiled as they ran across the pasture to the truck. Thunder cracked across the sky, and the first big drops of rain came stinging down on them just as they dashed inside and closed the doors after them.

Shelby was exhilarated and out of breath. Her eyes shone as she smiled at Parker across the front seat.

"You look happy," he said as he wiped a drop of rain from her cheek with his thumb.

"I know I shouldn't be, but I am. For the first time in..." She shrugged her shoulders. "I can't remember how long."

"Good." He looked at her a moment longer, then turned the key in the ignition and headed for home. By the time they got there, the rain was hammering the earth. He parked as close to the house as he could, and the two of them made a run for the porch.

The police officer had been waiting for them and pushed open the front door. Lightning streaked across the sky followed by an earsplitting roar of thunder.

"Nice night for a walk," he said, tongue-in-cheek.

It wasn't quite night yet, but it had grown so dark it might as well have been.

Parker went upstairs and came back a minute later with two towels. He threw his over his shoulder, then stood in front of Shelby and gently dried her face.

Shelby put her hand over his. "Thank you," she said softly.

He smiled and gave her the towel.

Shelby went to a window to look outside while she toweled her hair. "Do you get these kinds of storms often?" She almost had to yell over the noise.

"Not really," Parker said from just behind her as he looked outside too. "I'm not going to complain about this one, though. We desperately need the rain. And wait until you smell how sweet the air is when it's all over."

Shelby nodded, still watching the storm.

"What time is it?" Parker asked the officer.

"Five-thirty."

"I didn't realize it was that late. I have to get some paperwork done, Shelby. You're welcome to join me in my study if you want."

She turned around. "Thank you. I might as well try to reorganize my notes for the article. They're really an incredible mess."

"You get your things and I'll make some sandwiches for us to eat while we work."

Shelby ran upstairs and pulled the loose sheets of papers, torn scraps and intact notebooks from her suitcase, putting everything into a pile and then carrying it downstairs to the small study. There was only one desk, but even if there'd been two, it would have been enough room. Shelby sat on the floor and started spreading her things out around her.

When Parker came in carrying a tray with sandwiches and iced tea, he hunkered down next to her and looked over the ruins. "That guy really did a job on your work, didn't he?"

Shelby looked at it and sighed. "It's going to take me forever to piece it together."

"Maybe you should just start over."

"I can with some things, of course, but not with everything. I'll have to pick and choose as I go along, get court transcripts and redo some interviews."

Parker took one of the sandwiches and a glass of tea, and carried it to his desk.

"Where's the officer?" she asked, looking up and past him toward the other room.

"He's going to stay in the living room."

Within minutes, the two of them were absorbed in their work nearly to the exclusion of everything else. Hours went by without their realizing it.

When the phone rang, Shelby jumped and put her hand over her heart. There was still thunder, but she'd grown accustomed to it. The phone was an unexpected noise, and one she'd grown wary of.

Parker listened for a long time before speaking. "Do you know where he is?"

He listened some more.

"Why haven't the New York authorities picked him up for questioning?"

"Who?" Shelby asked urgently, knowing he was talking about her attacker.

Parker raised his finger, indicating that he'd tell her in just a minute.

"I'll be right there. Do you want me to bring Shelby?"

He listened.

"All right. Goodbye."

"What is it?" Shelby asked when he hung up.

"The police. They think they might have a lead on Diane Lyle's mystery caller."

"And mine, presumably."

"They think he might also have been her lover."

"Who is it?"

"Your editor—and hers."

Shelby's lips parted softly in surprise. "Peter? Peter Krist? Oh, come on, he's one of the nicest men in the world. And he's very married."

"Which is undoubtedly the reason he didn't come forward when he had to have known that we were looking for him. I'm going to go to the courthouse to look at what the police have."

"Do you want me to come?"

"No. There's nothing you could do, anyway. I won't be gone very long. Stay here with the officer."

Shelby anxiously dug her teeth into her lower lip without realizing it.

"You're not frightened, are you?" Parker asked as he hunkered down on the floor in front of her.

"A little."

"I could call for another policeman," he said quietly.

Shelby suddenly felt silly. "No, that's all right. I'm sure I'll be fine. In fact, I think I might go to bed."

"Where's the gun?"

"In my room."

"Make sure you keep it near you."

She nodded.

His hand cupped her cheek. "When this is all over, you and I are going to have a long talk about our future."

Her eyes filled with distress. "Oh, Parker, I can't."

"Why?"

"It's not right."

"What isn't right? You're in love with me and you know it. I'm in love with you. What isn't right about that?"

"Eric is always going to be between us."

"Not if you don't let him."

"It's not a matter of my letting him. He's there."

"Honey," he said softly, "what you had with Eric is one thing. What we have together is something else entirely. You have to go on with your life and leave your past behind you. I'm your present and I'm your future. You know it in your heart."

She started to say something, but he gently touched her lips. "Not now. I want you to think about what I've said, and when your whisperer is caught and you don't have anything else to fear, then we'll talk. We'll talk until there's nothing left to say." He kissed her, then straightened and left the room.

Shelby got up and walked to the window. She was in over her head and didn't know what to do. There were so many conflicting feelings she couldn't sort out.

Parker turned in the doorway and looked back at her. He'd known her for such a short time, but couldn't imagine what life would be without her. "Don't let anything happen to her," he told the officer in the living room as he walked quickly past him, "or you'll answer to me."

"Don't worry about it, sir," the young man said confidently. "I've got my eyes and ears open."

Chapter Nine

Shelby was getting ready for bed when she thought she heard something. She listened carefully. Was that the telephone ringing? It was hard to tell over the rain and thunder.

She finished buttoning Parker's shirt and padded barefoot to her bedroom door to listen. It *was* the telephone. Why didn't the officer answer it?

No sooner did she have the thought than the ringing stopped. She waited a little longer, and when the officer didn't call her to the phone, she assumed it must have been for him.

She walked to her bed, stacked up the pillows and sank back against them. She wished Parker would get back so he could tell her what was going on. And wasn't this storm ever going to end? But in the meantime...

She took a deep breath and slowly exhaled, then started to read a book she'd brought up from the library.

The bedside lamp flickered.

Shelby's eyes flew to it and stayed there.

It flickered again.

Downstairs she could hear the telephone ring again, and this time it kept on ringing.

Her heart started to beat faster. She set the book aside and reached into the end table for the gun just as the light flickered again and went out.

Now her heart was pounding. She rose from the bed, clutching the gun, and started for her door. Opening it a crack, she listened intently and wished to heaven the rain would stop so she could hear better. The light that had been on in the hallway was now out. It was probably the storm, she told herself.

Moving out into the hallway, she pressed her back against the wall as she moved toward the stairs, alert, straining to see in the dark.

Lightning flashed through the sky. Its brightness flared through the window and lit the hall like a camera flash.

Then it was dark again.

Shelby inched her way to the stairs and stood like a statue, listening. The rain wasn't so loud now, and the thunder was more a distant rumble than a crash.

Again lightning flared, bathing the stairway and downstairs hallway in a flickering white light. There was no one there but Shelby.

She started down the steps, stopping at every creak of wood, listening for anything that was out of place.

She desperately wanted to call out for the policeman, but something told her not to.

She was sure there was someone in the house with her. She could feel his presence. And it wasn't a friendly one.

Lightning flickered.

She hurried down the rest of the steps while she could see them and hugged the wall as she rounded the corner into the living room. Out of breath, her heart pounding against her rib cage, she searched the darkness with her eyes.

"I've been waiting for you, Shelby," a man whispered.

She raised the gun in shaking hands, but she couldn't see anything. It was impossible to tell where the whisper was coming from. It was such an undefined sound.

"You thought your boyfriend would protect you, didn't you? But as you see, he can't. No one can."

Shelby's mind raced. If she couldn't see him, then he couldn't see her. She moved quietly along the wall.

A match flared in a far corner of the room as the man casually lit a cigarette. Its light played eerily over his face, but she couldn't see his features. He dropped the match, and it fell halfway to the floor before extinguishing itself. The pungent smell of tobacco drifted through the room.

She raised the gun and aimed it at the corner. "I have a gun," she said, trying desperately not to sound afraid. "I'll use it if I have to."

The cigarette glowed bright red and then faded. "You could never shoot me."

"I can and I will if you leave me no choice. Where is the officer who was here? What did you do to him?" She kept her eyes on the glowing cigarette.

"He's having a nice little nap."

The man had moved to the left. He must have set the cigarette down. Shelby turned to where she thought he was, still holding the gun out in front of her. "Did you hurt him?"

"Let's just say that he's going to have quite a headache when he finally wakes up."

Lightning flashed, but she couldn't see the man. It was too quick, no longer than it took to blink.

Please, Parker, come home, she pleaded in her thoughts. *Please.*

"Shelby, Shelby, Shelby," he whispered, "you've brought this all on yourself, you know. It's all your fault."

He'd moved again, closer to her.

She didn't say anything.

The lights in the living room flickered and went on. Shelby found herself looking at a face she knew all too well.

"I guess the power company is working overtime," the man said with a smile. "It's just as well. It's time you knew."

"Charles?" she said in shock, her gun forgotten as her hand fell to her side. It slipped from her fingers and landed on the carpet with a soft thud. "You?"

"Charles? You?" he mimicked her words. "You amaze me, Shelby." He was no longer whispering. "I was such a nonentity to you that it never even occurred to you that it might be me."

"Why are you doing this?"

"At first, it was because you looked so much like Diane."

She swallowed hard. "Diane?"

"I loved her. She let me love her. She wanted me to love her. And then she betrayed me."

"I'm not Diane."

"You're no better than she was. Always so nice, so caring. Making me love you, just like she did. And then betraying me with another man."

"Charles, we were just friends."

"I didn't want your friendship. I wanted you to love me."

"I didn't know."

He raised his gun and aimed it at her. "I killed Diane and now I'm going to kill you. Neither of you deserve to live."

Shelby was hanging on to her composure by a thread. "Charles, don't do this. Talk to me."

"I'm through talking. Goodbye, Shelby."

In that moment, as she could see him squeezing the trigger, Shelby knew she was going to die. She looked straight at him, unflinching, and waited with as much dignity as she could.

"No!"

Parker's voice seemed to come out of nowhere. Charles whirled around and fired his gun. Another shot came from the policeman behind Parker and Charles fell to the ground.

But Shelby wasn't looking at Charles. She was looking in horror at the red stain that was spreading across the front of Parker's shirt. He looked straight into her eyes and staggered.

"Oh, my God!" she screamed, running forward and catching him in her arms as he fell.

The policeman kicked Charles's gun out of the way and checked the man for a pulse. "I'll call for an ambulance for Parker," he said, rising. "This other guy isn't going to be needing one. He's not going to be needing anything anymore."

Shelby looked at the still form of the man who'd been stalking her.

"Where's the other officer who was here?" the policeman asked as he looked around.

"I don't know." Shelby stretched her legs out and rested Parker's head on her lap. "Please hurry up and get the ambulance. Parker?" she said softly as she stroked his hair. "Parker?"

He opened his eyes and looked up at her. "Are you hurt, Shelby?"

She shook her head as tears streamed down her face.

He let out a long breath and grimaced. "I tried to call you. When no one answered the phone, I called the police and got here as fast as I could."

The policeman came back in with a big bath towel. "Ambulance is on the way," he said as he knelt next to Parker and ripped open his shirt. "I found the other officer. He's got a nasty knock on the head, but he's going to be okay."

Shelby looked at the wound. It was hard to see exactly where it was because of all the blood, but it seemed to be in the right chest area.

"I'm having a hard time breathing," Parker said weakly.

The officer nodded as he pressed one of the towels to his chest. "The bullet might have nicked a lung."

Shelby gently cupped the side of Parker's face in her hand and gazed down at him.

He tried to smile reassuringly. "I'll be all right."

Several more policemen walked in and started wandering around the living room.

"This is all my fault," Shelby said, her voice trembling with emotion.

"Shelby, I told you before that you have no control over what crazy people do." Parker took a painful breath.

"Please don't talk anymore. Just lie here quietly until the ambulance comes." She could hear a siren in the distance.

Let him be all right, she prayed silently.

Shelby paced back and forth in the waiting room of the hospital.

"Shelby!"

She turned abruptly to find Danny running toward her, tears streaming down his face. "Is my daddy all right?"

Kneeling, she held out her arms and caught him, holding him close. "He will be, Danny."

"What happened? Rosa wouldn't tell me."

Shelby looked up and into Rosa's distressed eyes.

"A man who wanted to hurt me ended up hurting your father instead when he came to help me."

"So my dad is kind of a hero?"

Shelby pushed his hair away from his damp face. "Your dad is very much a hero."

"Can I see him now?"

"I'm afraid not yet, sweetheart. The doctors are still taking care of him."

"When will they be finished?"

"I don't know."

"Well, I'm gonna stay here until they are."

It was three o'clock in the morning. Shelby rose, her hand still on Danny's shoulder. "What do you think, Rosa?"

"We'll stay. I could use some coffee. What about you?"

"I don't want anything, thank you."

"I'll be right back."

Shelby took Danny by the hand and led him to a couch. As they sat down, she put her arm around Danny and held him against her side. "He really is going to be fine, Danny."

He nodded but didn't say anything.

"He has to be," she said softly.

"Parker. Wake up, Parker," Shelby pleaded with him. "Look at me." She held his hand in hers, stroking his fingers. "Come on. You can do it. The doctor says you're going to be fine."

He could hear her, but she sounded so far away.

Shelby rested her cool hand on his forehead, then leaned over and rested her cheek against his. "I'm so sorry," she said softly against his ear. "I never meant for anything to happen to you."

Parker knew she was holding his hand. He wanted to squeeze her fingers to let her know that he was aware, but he couldn't. Not yet. He drifted off beyond reach again.

Parker opened his eyes and found himself looking at a white ceiling. Sunlight streamed in through open blinds. He turned his head ever so slightly and saw Shelby sitting beside him, staring at his hand, stroking his fingers.

He curled his fingers around hers.

Shelby looked at his face, and when she saw his blue eyes gazing back at her, she smiled in relief. "Hello."

He smiled also. "Hello. What happened?"

"You got shot."

"I remember that, but it's about the last thing I remember."

"You lost a lot of blood and you had to have surgery to repair some lung damage. Everyone's been very worried."

"You're **all** right?" he asked.

"Thanks to you, I'm fine. I still can't believe it was Charles. I never would have guessed."

"Where is he now?"

"He got shot, too. I'm afraid he didn't make it. Parker, he told me that he killed Diane."

"Did he tell you why?"

"Because he loved her and she betrayed him."

"With her editor, no doubt. He confirmed that night that he'd had an affair with her."

"And Charles thought I was having an affair with you. That's why I suddenly became his enemy." Her eyes stung with tears.

"Oh, Shelby, don't do that to yourself. What happened to him isn't your fault."

"I should have seen . . ."

"You could only see what he let you see. He chose his end, not you." His gaze moved over her distressed face and grew tender. "Come here."

"What?"

"Lean toward me."

She did, and Parker raised his hand to gently wipe the tears from her cheeks. "I'm glad your nightmare is over. Now you can start thinking about us."

Her heart caught. "Not yet."

He looked at her without speaking.

"There are some things I need to clear up in my life first. Now that you're better, I'm going back to Vermont."

"Eric?"

She nodded. "I can't be with you yet. Please understand."

"Are you coming back to me, Shelby? Or am I going to lose you to your ghosts?"

"I need time."

"All right. But while you're in Vermont confronting your past, remember that I love you."

Chapter Ten

A month had gone by since Shelby had left Texas. The article was finished. It had turned out to be more of a story of her personal pilgrimage than about the trial, though it all seemed to flow together. At any rate, it had been received by her editor with enthusiasm.

And now it was her last day in Vermont. It was a beautiful day. Just a hint of a breeze. Shelby kneeled in front of Eric's grave and gazed at his headstone. "Hello, Eric," she said softly as she set a small bouquet against the marble. "A lot has happened to me since the last time I was here. I've been very confused since you died, but I'm not any longer. I've met a wonderful man. You would have liked him. I want to marry him, if he'll have me." She smiled. "I think I must be his **worst** nightmare. He's such a sane, stable man, and I've been a little crazy lately.''

She sighed. ''The thing is, Eric, I can't go to him freely until I put my life in order; until I deal with the past. I want you to know that I love you. You'll always be in my heart. But I'm ready to go on with my life now.'' She slipped the wedding band from her finger. ''I'm going to leave this with you.'' She pressed it into the earth where the grass met the headstone, until the gold was just beneath the surface.

She traced his name with her fingertip. ''Goodbye, Eric.''

When she got back to her car, Katy was standing there. ''Where did you come from?'' Shelby asked.

''You haven't returned any of my calls. When I did get you, you didn't want to talk. I showed up at your house this morning, and when you weren't there, I thought I'd try here. Would you mind telling me what's going on?''

Shelby hugged her friend. ''Oh, Katy, I'm sorry, but I've had a lot on my mind. I just wanted to be left alone to sort through things.''

''And have you?''

''Oh, yes.'' A soft smile touched her lips.

''And would this sorting you've been doing have anything to do with that Texan you told me about?''

''It has everything to do with him.''

Katy smiled, too. It was impossible to see her friend's happiness and not be happy for her. ''So when do I get to meet this Mr. Wonderful?''

''I have to see if he still wants me first.''

''You think he might be having second thoughts?''

"I don't know. I've caused him a lot of trouble. Much more than he ever bargained for. More than he deserved." She looked at her watch. "I have to leave for the airport."

Katy hugged her. "Good luck."

Shelby climbed into her car.

"Call me as soon as you can," Katy said as she leaned in the open window.

"I will."

Shelby drove down the dusty road of Parker's ranch. It was just about sunset. There were butterflies in her stomach. She had no idea what kind of reception she was going to receive.

Rosa was on the porch when Shelby pulled up and parked her car. Shelby got out and started up the steps as Rosa came down them. She found herself swallowed in Rosa's arms. "I knew you'd come back," the housekeeper said.

"Where's Parker?"

"He's out in one of the pastures working."

"Already? What about his wound?"

"He's still healing, but he's much better. Unfortunately, he's never been very good at just sitting around."

"I need to see him, Rosa."

"Then get back in your car and follow the road for another mile. You'll come to a fork. Go to the left. He should be somewhere along there."

"Thank you."

Shelby got back behind her steering wheel, took a deep breath, and headed out. She did exactly what

Rosa had told her, and sure enough, there Parker was, much the same way he'd been the last time she'd visited him in his fields. His shirt was off as he worked at hammering a nail into a wooden gate he'd erected. He was thinner than he had been.

She stopped the car about twenty yards away and got out. Parker stopped his hammering and looked at her, but made no move toward her. Licking suddenly dry lips, she started walking and didn't stop until she stood in front of him, her eyes searching his face for some sign of what he was thinking. "Hello, Parker."

He inclined his dark head. "Shelby."

"I'm glad to see you're so much better than you were the last time I saw you in the hospital."

The muscle in his jaw moved.

"I missed you."

He still didn't say anything.

"I love you."

His blue eyes grew more intense. Though he knew— and had known—that she did, it was the first time she'd said the words to him.

"I made peace with my past and now I'm here—if you still want me."

"If I still want you?" Parker reached out and pulled her into the strong circle of his arms. "If? I've never wanted anyone more. I wasn't sure you were coming back."

"You could have come after me."

Parker held her away from him and looked into her eyes. "No, I couldn't. What you had to do, you had to do alone. God knows I wanted to come after you, but it would have been wrong. I had to give you the freedom to come back to me on your own.''

"I love you,'' she said again. It was wonderful, not just to say the words, but to allow herself to have the feelings. No guilt. No guilt ever again.

"I love you, too. Marry me, Shelby. Right now. Today.''

"You don't have to marry me. I'll be here even if you don't.''

He touched her cheek with a gentle hand. "I want to marry you. I've never wanted anything more. I want to spend the rest of my life with you.''

Shelby raised her hand to his. Their fingers twined together. Parker suddenly held her hand out and looked at her bare ring finger. Shelby looked at it, too. "I was so afraid to let myself love you. I wouldn't even let myself think about it, much less feel it. But that night when Charles shot you and I thought you might die, I knew. There was no more denial. You meant more to me than my own life. The thought that I might lose you was almost more than I could bear. You mean everything to me, Parker.''

He cupped her face in both of his hands and kissed her long and hard. "I'm so glad you're back,'' he said, leaning his forehead against hers. "Danny would never have forgiven me if you'd gone away for good.''

"I missed him.''

"He's looking forward to having you for his mother.''

Shelby smiled. It lit her whole face and warmed the man holding her in his arms.

"You're going to be a wonderful mother." He lowered his mouth to hers.

Shelby abandoned herself to him completely. No regrets. No more questions.

Just herself and the man she loved.

Epilogue

Shelby lay on her stomach, her chin resting on the palm of her hand, watching her husband sleep. Dark beard shadowed his cheeks, as it did every morning. He seemed so peaceful—but then he was always that way.

Was there ever a man so sure of himself? So sure of the two of them together?

She smiled.

Parker opened his eyes and looked drowsily at her. A slow smile curved his mouth. "Good morning."

"Morning."

He reached out and pulled her on top of him. "Have I told you how much I love waking up with you every morning?"

"Um-hmm."

He ran his hand down the curve of her back and pressed her against him. "You feel good. What are you thinking?"

"That I love you. I never thought I could feel this way."

"You wouldn't let yourself."

"Until you made me."

He pushed her hair away from her face. "No more guilt?"

"No. Just happiness and the most complete contentment I've ever felt. You and Danny are my world, and I wouldn't have it any other way."

Parker's gaze moved over her face, lovely even at this early hour. He sensed that there was more going on than what she was saying. "What is it?"

"You know me too well."

"I wonder sometimes if you can ever know the one you love too well. What aren't you telling me?"

Shelby looked into his eyes. "You've never said anything about our having children."

"I didn't want to pressure you. I thought we'd just take one day at a time."

"Well, I'm ready. I want to have your child, Parker. I want to give Danny a little brother or sister."

There was a sudden light in his blue eyes. "Are you sure, Shelby?"

"Oh, yes. I've never been more sure of anything in my life, except the way I feel about you."

Parker wrapped her in his arms and held her. Nothing could have told him more eloquently how completely she'd given herself to him.

He turned her onto her back and settled her gently against the pillows. "I love you, Shelby Kincaid."

His kiss was warm and deep; his touch gentle and sure as he found his way over every inch of her body, taking her to heights she'd never dreamed existed.

*   *   *   *   *

COMING NEXT MONTH

AVAILABLE THIS MONTH:

Take 4 bestselling love stories FREE

Plus get a FREE surprise gift!

Special Limited-time Offer

Mail to
Silhouette Reader Service™
3010 Walden Avenue
P.O. Box 1867
Buffalo, N.Y. 14269-1867

YES! Please send me 4 free Silhouette Romance™ novels and my free surprise gift. Then send me 6 brand-new novels every month, which I will receive months before they appear in bookstores. Bill me at the low price of $2.25 each—a savings of 25¢ apiece off cover prices. There are no shipping, handling or other hidden costs. I understand that accepting the books and gift places me under no obligation ever to buy any books. I can always return a shipment and cancel at any time. Even if I never buy another book from Silhouette, the 4 free books and the surprise gift are mine to keep forever.

215 BPA AC7N

Name	(PLEASE PRINT)
Address	Apt. No.
City	State	Zip

This offer is limited to one order per household and not valid to present Silhouette Romance™ subscribers. Terms and prices are subject to change. Sales tax applicable in N.Y.

SROM-BPA2DR   © 1990 Harlequin Enterprises Limited

WRITTEN IN THE STARS

HE'S OUT OF THIS WORLD

in

ARC OF THE ARROW

Could Sagittarian R. G. Travers have finally met his match? Find out in Rita Rainville's ARC OF THE ARROW, the WRITTEN IN THE STARS title for December 1991—only from Silhouette Romance!

Brandy Cochran didn't *really* believe that R.G. was an alien—no matter what her zany Aunt Tillie said. But she did admit that his kiss put her in orbit!

ARC OF THE ARROW by Rita Rainville... coming from Silhouette Romance this December. It's WRITTEN IN THE STARS!

 Silhouette Romance®

This is the season of giving, and Silhouette proudly offers you its sixth annual Christmas collection.

SILHOUETTE

Christmas Stories

1991

Experience the joys of a holiday romance and treasure these heart-warming stories by four award-winning Silhouette authors:

Phyllis Halldorson—"A Memorable Noel"
Peggy Webb—"I Heard the Rabbits Singing"
Naomi Horton—"Dreaming of Angels"
Heather Graham Pozzessere—"The Christmas Bride"

Discover this yuletide celebration—sit back and enjoy Silhouette's Christmas gift of love.

SILHOUETTE®
OFFICIAL SWEEPSTAKES
RULES

NO PURCHASE NECESSARY

1. To enter, complete an Official Entry Form or 3"× 5" index card by hand-printing, in plain block letters, your complete name, address, phone number and age, and mailing it to: Silhouette Fashion A Whole New You Sweepstakes, P.O. Box 9056, Buffalo, NY 14269-9056.

   No responsibility is assumed for lost, late or misdirected mail. Entries must be sent separately with first class postage affixed, and be received no later than December 31, 1991 for eligibility.

2. Winners will be selected by D.L. Blair, Inc., an independent judging organization whose decisions are final, in random drawings to be held on January 30, 1992 in Blair, NE at 10:00 a.m. from among all eligible entries received.

3. The prizes to be awarded and their approximate retail values are as follows: Grand Prize — A brand-new Ford Explorer 4×4 plus a trip for two (2) to Hawaii, including round-trip air transportation, six (6) nights hotel accommodation, a $1,400 meal/spending money stipend and $2,000 cash toward a new fashion wardrobe (approximate value: $28,000) or $15,000 cash; two (2) Second Prizes — A trip to Hawaii, including round-trip air transportation, six (6) nights hotel accommodation, a $1,400 meal/spending money stipend and $2,000 cash toward a new fashion wardrobe (approximate value: $11,000) or $5,000 cash; three (3) Third Prizes — $2,000 cash toward a new fashion wardrobe. All prizes are valued in U.S. currency. Travel award air transportation is from the commercial airport nearest winner's home. Travel is subject to space and accommodation availability, and must be completed by June 30, 1993. Sweepstakes offer is open to residents of the U.S. and Canada who are 21 years of age or older as of December 31, 1991, except residents of Puerto Rico, employees and immediate family members of Torstar Corp., its affiliates, subsidiaries, and all agencies, entities and persons connected with the use, marketing, or conduct of this sweepstakes. All federal, state, provincial, municipal and local laws apply. Offer void wherever prohibited by law. Taxes and/or duties, applicable registration and licensing fees, are the sole responsibility of the winners. Any litigation within the province of Quebec respecting the conduct and awarding of a prize may be submitted to the Régie des loteries et courses du Québec. All prizes will be awarded; winners will be notified by mail. No substitution of prizes is permitted.

4. Potential winners must sign and return any required Affidavit of Eligibility/Release of Liability within 30 days of notification. In the event of noncompliance within this time period, the prize may be awarded to an alternate winner. Any prize or prize notification returned as undeliverable may result in the awarding of that prize to an alternate winner. By acceptance of their prize, winners consent to use of their names, photographs or their likenesses for purposes of advertising, trade and promotion on behalf of Torstar Corp. without further compensation. Canadian winners must correctly answer a time-limited arithmetical question in order to be awarded a prize.

5. For a list of winners (available after 3/31/92), send a separate stamped, self-addressed envelope to: Silhouette Fashion A Whole New You Sweepstakes, P.O. Box 4665, Blair, NE 68009.

PREMIUM OFFER TERMS

To receive your gift, complete the Offer Certificate according to directions. Be certain to enclose the required number of "Fashion A Whole New You" proofs of product purchase (which are found on the last page of every specially marked "Fashion A Whole New You" Silhouette or Harlequin romance novel). Requests must be received no later than December 31, 1991. Limit: four (4) gifts per name, family, group, organization or address. Items depicted are for illustrative purposes only and may not be exactly as shown. Please allow 6 to 8 weeks for receipt of order. Offer good while quantities of gifts last. In the event an ordered gift is no longer available, you will receive a free, previously unpublished Silhouette or Harlequin book for every proof of purchase you have submitted with your request, plus a refund of the postage and handling charge you have included. Offer good in the U.S. and Canada only.

SLFW - SWPR

SILHOUETTE® OFFICIAL SWEEPSTAKES ENTRY FORM

4-FWSRS-4

Complete and return this Entry Form immediately – the more entries you submit, the better your chances of winning!

- Entries must be received by **December 31, 1991**.
- A Random draw will take place on **January 30, 1992**.
- No purchase necessary.

Yes, I want to win a FASHION A WHOLE NEW YOU Sensuous and Adventurous prize from Silhouette:

Name _____ Telephone _____ Age _____

Address _____

City _____ State _____ Zip _____

Return Entries to: **Silhouette FASHION A WHOLE NEW YOU,**
P.O. Box 9056, Buffalo, NY 14269-9056   © 1991 Harlequin Enterprises Limited

PREMIUM OFFER

To receive your free gift, send us the required number of proofs-of-purchase from any specially marked FASHION A WHOLE NEW YOU Silhouette or Harlequin Book with the Offer Certificate properly completed, plus a check or money order (do not send cash) to cover postage and handling payable to Silhouette FASHION A WHOLE NEW YOU Offer. We will send you the specified gift.

OFFER CERTIFICATE

Item	A. SENSUAL DESIGNER VANITY BOX COLLECTION (set of 4) (Suggested Retail Price $60.00)	B. ADVENTUROUS TRAVEL COSMETIC CASE SET (set of 3) (Suggested Retail Price $25.00)
# of proofs-of-purchase	18	12
Postage and Handling	$3.50	$2.95
Check one	☐	☐

Name _____

Address _____

City _____ State _____ Zip _____

Mail this certificate, designated number of proofs-of-purchase and check or money order for postage and handling to: **Silhouette FASHION A WHOLE NEW YOU Gift Offer,** P.O. Box 9057, Buffalo, NY 14269-9057. Requests must be received by December 31, 1991.

ONE PROOF-OF-PURCHASE

4-FWSRP-4

To collect your fabulous free gift you must include the necessary number of proofs-of-purchase with a properly completed Offer Certificate.

© 1991 Harlequin Enterprises Limited

See previous page for details.